NIPPED IN THE BUD

SHEILA CONNOLLY

WHEELER PUBLISHING
A part of Gale, a Cengage Company

Farmington Hills, Mich • San Francisco • New York • Waterville, Maine
Meriden, Conn • Mason, Ohio • Chicago

Copyright © 2018 by Sheila Connolly.
An Orchard Mystery.
Wheeler Publishing, a part of Gale, a Cengage Company.

Wheeler Publishing Large Print Cozy Mystery.
The text of this Large Print edition is unabridged.
Other aspects of the book may vary from the original edition.
Set in 16 pt. Plantin.

LIBRARY OF CONGRESS CIP DATA ON FILE.
CATALOGUING IN PUBLICATION FOR THIS BOOK
IS AVAILABLE FROM THE LIBRARY OF CONGRESS

ISBN-13: 978-1-4328-6646-4 (softcover alk. paper)

Published in 2019 by arrangement with Beyond the Page Publishing, LLC

Printed in the United States of America
1 2 3 4 5 6 7 23 22 21 20 19

NIPPED IN THE BUD

1

Meg Corey — *oops, now Chapin,* she reminded herself yet again — stared out the window over the sink, her hands immersed in dirty dishes and soapy water. Outside the window lay an almost monochrome winter landscape — naked dark brown trunks, scattered drifts of cinnamon-colored leaves, a few evergreens, punctuated by patches of old snow. Even the grass was brownish. Her two goats, Dorcas and Isabel, had given up trying to graze and were chomping on the hay she'd left out for them. She'd bring them into the barn before it got dark.

Too bad her orchard lay on the opposite side of the house, running up the hill. She thought, not for the first time, of flipping the layout of the kitchen, moving the sink to the other side so she could keep her eye on the apple trees as the fruit grew over the summer and fall. There wasn't much to see right now, and the currently bare branches taunted her: it was pruning time, all the experts said, but she hadn't even begun. She liked to prune, cutting out the dead branches and clearing the space between branches and around the trunks to allow the apples to flourish, even though she felt guilty every time she "killed" a branch. Still, it was necessary to give the apples the best chance to prosper. And if she burnt the branches in the fireplace, they gave off a nice scent.

"Are you washing those dishes or soaking them?" Her relatively new husband, Seth Chapin, came up behind her and wrapped his arms around her waist.

Meg looked down at the scummy pool of gray water in front of her. "I forget. Maybe they need to soak a while longer." She dried her hands on a convenient dish towel, then pivoted to face Seth. "I'm so busy most of the year that I forget what to do when I have free time. I've even done the taxes already — early." Meg's financial background made her the logical choice to deal with tax filings, even though both she and Seth managed their own small businesses.

"How'd we do this year?"

"Not bad. Better than last year. But the good weather helped. You have any projects going?"

"Winter's my slow time too. Most people don't want me tearing out walls and replacing windows when it's below freezing outside. Of course, that means once it warms up I'll be crazy busy." Seth had started out as a plumber working with his father, but after his father's death he had shifted to his first love, renovation of local houses with the goal of preserving as much of the original structure and architectural detail as possible. His reputation had grown steadily in the Pioneer Valley, so he kept busy in fair weather. There were plenty of colonial houses in the area, so he wouldn't run out of jobs anytime soon.

"What's Larry doing?" he asked. "I haven't seen much of him."

"Well, he arrived kind of late in the season when he took over from Bree, so I think he's been polishing his apple skills with Christopher while things are slow. Has he talked with you about the tiny house?"

When Meg had taken over the orchard, Bree had already been working there, guided by Christopher Ramsdell, a professor at UMass Amherst. Since Meg had no idea what her cash situation would be, she'd offered Bree the title of orchard manager as well as a room in the house, which had worked out well for everyone. But Bree was a long way away, and Meg and Seth had gotten married and they didn't feel right about having Bree's replacement, Larry Bennett, live in the same house. When they'd begun considering alternatives, the somewhat trendy concept of a "tiny house" had come up, and Larry had seized on it as ideal for his needs, which were few, but which definitely included privacy.

"We discussed the basic requirements a while back. We've drawn up some plans, but we're waiting for the weather to warm up a bit. Shouldn't take long to put together, once we get started."

"So he's still staying at your house up the hill?"

"For now. I get the feeling he doesn't much like having roommates, though. He'd rather have his own space, no matter how small."

"He does seem like a real loner," Meg agreed. "Are Christopher and your mother still, uh . . . ?" Meg was reluctant to pin a name on their relationship, even though they'd been — seeing each other? dating? — for several months now. Seth's mother, Lydia, had been a widow for years, and Christopher a widower, but somehow they'd mutually decided they were tired of being alone. Meg was happy for them both — and the idea of having internationally renowned pomologist Christopher only minutes away was reassuring, especially since he was the person who had kept the old orchard healthy for decades. Besides which, he was delightful company.

She turned back to the mess of dishes in the sink but found herself staring out the window once again. "Oh, look — it's a fox. I haven't seen many around here."

"Where?"

Meg pointed out across the meadow. "He's hard to miss with that lovely red coat. Or is it a she?"

"Can't really tell from here. They've been rare in the area for a while. The foxes used to be a real nuisance to anyone who kept chickens, but fewer and fewer people do now."

"What else do they eat?"

"Birds, small rodents. I'm no expert."

"It wouldn't be hard to know more than I do — I've been a city girl most of my life. Can I assume they don't eat apples?"

"You'd have noticed by now. And they don't climb trees, as far as I know. They're mainly carnivorous. The only thing to worry about is illness — they can get rabies, and sometimes you see one with mange."

"Like they lose their fur?"

"Pretty much. Mange is a kind of infection caused by mites. It's itchy, and the foxes' skin can get infected and then they can get parasites. Sometimes they die from starvation since the parasites are sucking up all their nutrition."

"That sounds awful. Does mange spread? Should we worry about Max getting it?" Max was the golden retriever they shared, after Seth had adopted him. Max had never met another animal or human that he didn't like, so most likely he'd try to get close to a fox, which could be a problem on more than one level.

"Apparently mange doesn't affect dogs and cats. Or goats, if you're wondering."

"Is there anything to be done about it? For the foxes, I mean?"

"If you see it early enough, there are drugs that can kill off the mites. You can leave out food injected with the medication, which seems to work. Assuming you want to keep the foxes around?"

"I think they're pretty, but I wouldn't plan to make a pet of one. Is it a problem locally?"

"Not that I'm aware of, but an infected fox could wander into the neighborhood at any time."

"Great. One more thing to worry about."

"I wouldn't put it high on your list, Meg. Unless it's hunting season."

There was a fox-hunting season? "Which is when?"

"Now. It ends at the end of this month."

"How come I haven't heard of this before?" Meg demanded indignantly.

"Because Granford is not very good hunting territory — there are better places for serious hunters in this area. Of course, there are always a few farmers who go after rats with a shotgun, because they eat their grain, but none of our closest neighbors keeps animals, much less shoots at pests."

"Good to know, I guess. So I don't need a bulletproof vest when I go out to feed the goats?"

"I think you'll be safe. And I would have told you if I thought you needed one."

"Do you need a permit to own a gun?" Meg asked.

"This is Massachusetts — what do you think?"

"I'll assume that means yes. It seems you need a permit for almost everything in this state from what you've told me about construction, old or new." Somehow she'd finished the dishes while they talked, and they were draining. Meg dried her hands and turned back to Seth. "Want to take a walk before it gets too dark?"

"Okay. Any place in particular?"

"Just out. Like I said, I feel restless when there's nothing I have to do. It's not raining or snowing, and I'll have to get the goats into the barn before dark, so why not go now? We can look over the apple trees and see how much pruning we'll have to do. And you can tell me about your latest plans for the tiny house. And walk Max."

"You are something else," Seth said, laughing. "You've got a foot-long to-do list for your free time."

"Some people would call that an efficient use of time," Meg replied, but she wasn't troubled by it. Neither one of them was a lazy person, which was probably why they fit so well together. Well, one of the reasons — there were plenty of others.

Ten minutes later, wrapped with cold-weather gear and accompanied by an eager Max, they made it out the back door. Meg inhaled deeply. "It smells so clean," she said.

"Smells like snow to me," Seth said.

"You can tell?"

"Kind of. But I checked the weather report. Flurries only, it said, but I've got a delivery of lumber coming and I need to get it stashed in the barn."

"Then walk faster, if you want to get any

exercise in. Oh, wait — I might as well put the goats in the barn now, since we may be a while."

That task was quickly accomplished. Afterward, despite good intentions, they didn't hurry. Without discussing it they headed for the top of the hill that the orchard occupied, then stopped to admire the view. The house stood solid and four-square near the road, as it had for over two hundred years. The rows of mature apple trees straggled their way down the slope of the hill. Off to the north, a few acres of young trees stood in neater rows; she and Seth had planted them together before they were married, but they were small and probably wouldn't bear any apples for at least a year, certainly not enough to take to market. But that little orchard had been a commitment to their shared future, and Meg had chosen heirloom varieties, suited to the region. They might not bring in as much money as the better-known standard varieties, but Meg wanted them in order to preserve their history.

Turning to their left, Meg could see Seth's former house, where Larry was living, and beyond that the roofline of what had been his family home, where his mother had stayed after the death of Seth's father. The farm Meg and Seth were living on, which Meg had inherited, was the only producing land on this side of the old road — the rest were now residences only, lovingly maintained. The town was beyond their sight, though at the crest of the hill they could hear the sound of passing cars on the local highway.

It all looked lovely and peaceful in the approaching dusk, and Meg leaned against Seth — her husband! — and allowed herself to simply relax and enjoy the view. Even Max was still, as if sharing their mood.

It didn't last. Meg heard the sound of a gunshot. She couldn't distinguish between kinds of guns, so she looked at Seth. "Rifle," he said. "A little too close for comfort. There are regulations about discharging firearms near settled areas, which this is. Plus, the light's fading fast, so it would be hard to see your target."

"Do you have to report it to someone?"

"Wouldn't be much use if I can't identify the shooter. I'll let the police know that somebody isn't following the rules."

Alert to the sound of any possible hunter, Seth hadn't been paying attention to Max, who suddenly took off toward where the gunshot had come from. "Damn it, Max, come back here," he yelled after the running dog.

Max ignored Seth and kept heading for the tree line. Meg told Seth, "You'd better go after him — we don't want that idiot hunter out there to think Max is a deer."

"Unfortunately you're right. Maybe you should go back to the house."

Which was exactly what she didn't want to do. "You have your cell phone?"

"Always. You?" When Meg nodded, Seth said, "I'll be back as soon as I catch up to that critter." Seth set off at a brisk run, but Max already had a head start. The dog vanished into the trees, and after a few seconds started barking loudly. At least if he kept that up no one would mistake him for a deer. Seth disappeared into the woods after him, calling his name.

Meg wavered. She wanted to wait until man and dog came back, safe and sound. But it was getting darker by the minute, and she was cold. She compromised by sitting down, her back against a tree, ready to wait. She looked up at the sky: no stars visible. Maybe Seth was right and there was snow coming — they hadn't had a lot this winter, so they were probably due for a storm. Massachusetts weather was getting increasingly unpredictable, and extreme as well: one week it could average sixty degrees, and the next week they'd get three feet of snow. Meg was still new enough to apple growing that she didn't know how the trees, established or new, would react to such inconsistent conditions, but there wasn't anything she could do about it.

Despite the cold, she was almost drowsing as darkness fell. The ringing of her cell phone, buried deep in one pocket of her coat, made her jump. She fished it out and checked the number: Seth's. "What's wrong?" she asked, jumping to the logical conclusions. "Did you lose Max?"

"Max is fine, and I put him on his leash. The problem is, there's a body. Human."

"That last gunshot we heard?"

"Probably. Blood's still fresh."

"Someone you know?"

"No, luckily. I've never seen her before."

"And the shooter?"

"Gone long before I arrived. Max made enough noise to drown out a herd of elk."

"What now?"

"I've called Art, but I'd better stay here so he can find the spot. You go back to the house, maybe make some coffee. I'm guessing it'll be a long night."

"Okay. Be careful, will you?"

"Of course. I've got someone to come home to now." He hung up.

Meg struggled to her feet, her legs stiff from sitting in the cold. Oddly enough she wasn't surprised: things had been too calm lately. A dead body would certainly change that.

2

Clearly she wasn't going to be able to sleep after what Seth had told her — not until he was back, safe and sound, and ideally with an explanation for why someone was dead in the woods. To occupy her mind while she trudged back toward the house she found herself wondering: was the body on her land? The house that was now hers had originally included over a hundred acres, back when it was a working farm. Now she had about fifteen acres of established trees in the older part of the orchard and another two or three of new plantings where her land and Seth's met. The property was ringed with old-growth trees, but she wasn't clear how far into those her land extended. Nor did she really know all the neighbors who lived beyond. Seth had said earlier that they weren't farmers, but that was about all she knew. Were there children living in those houses? Certainly if there were their parents should be alerted that there was someone who was careless with a weapon lurking among the trees.

Or else that someone had killed deliberately and disappeared under cover of darkness.

That was a chilling thought. Why there, why now? There were enough homes nearby that people would hear a shot, just as she had. That would at least narrow down the time the shooter was there. Had anyone seen someone exiting the woods? Getting into a car? Or maybe she was getting ahead of herself and it had been a suicide — although a rifle was not the easiest weapon to use for that. A handgun would have been a better choice. But again, why here? There were certainly more heavily wooded areas around, where a body might lie undetected for a long time.

She'd reached the house and let herself in — locking the door carefully behind her. After hanging up her down-filled coat, she filled the electric kettle so she could make coffee and scooped up her cat, Lolly, from her favorite perch on top of the refrigerator, and Meg tucked the furry bundle under her chin for a brief cuddle, until Lolly finally protested. Then she set about making the coffee, and wondered whether there were any cookies left. Which made her laugh: she was expecting a report on a death, suspicious or merely sad, and here she was thinking about hospitality. What does one serve at a police interrogation?

It could be a long wait. She knew the size and capabilities of the Granford Police Department, and she counted the Granford police chief Art Preston as a friend, after working together (along with Seth) on several unusual occurrences in Granford. At this time of night, in the dark, it would take Art a while to gather his staff for at least a preliminary assessment of the situation, and if there were anything suspicious about it, he'd probably be compelled to call in the state police from their headquarters in nearby Northampton. Which would make the immediate investigation even longer.

But she wasn't going to think about crawling into bed and trying to sleep, not while her husband was out in the cold with a dead body and members of more than one police force. She would sit in her warm kitchen like a faithful wife, keeping the coffee hot.

It was nearly midnight when she heard Seth's footsteps on the back steps. She could tell he was exhausted even without seeing him. When she opened the door, Max came bounding in; if he'd been a small child he would have been talking a mile a minute about what he'd seen (and smelled). He was probably the only one who'd had a good time tonight. Even as he twined around her legs, Meg reached out to Seth. "Come here." He did, without speaking, and held her for a few long moments.

"Was it awful?" she asked softly.

"It would have been worse if it had been a friend," he said.

"Still no ID for the body?"

"No."

Meg pulled away so she could look at Seth's face. "You said the victim was a woman?"

Seth nodded. "From what I could see she looked like she was in her thirties, maybe forty tops."

"Was it suicide?"

"Not unless she figured out how to fire a rifle into her back."

"That could be difficult," Meg agreed. "And I wouldn't choose to try it in a dark wood."

"Meg, I hope you never decide to try it, in a dark wood or anywhere else."

"I won't. I promise," she told him. Seth still looked haggard, although the color was coming back to his face. "Why don't you save all the details for tomorrow and go upstairs now?"

"As long as you come with me. Oh, we'd better set an wake-up alarm — Art Preston said he'd come by to get an official statement first thing, which will probably be early. And now that it's started to snow, that becomes more important, since I think I was the last person to see the scene before the snow started."

"Right now you look exhausted. Maybe Art and his men will know more by morning. Am I invited to sit in when you give Art your statement?"

"I hope so. Anyone who knows you will assume you would anyway."

Morning arrived too quickly — a dim gray morning. Seth was still sleeping, so Meg slid out of bed and tiptoed quietly to the bathroom. She peered out the window quickly: it had snowed only a little more during the night, but even two or three inches would mess up any forensic evidence at the death site. She smiled grimly at herself in the mirror — when had she started using terms like *forensic*? Since she'd been watching old reruns of crime shows, fighting to stay awake past nine o'clock in the evening. Farming was hard work, and she couldn't begin to count how many shows she had begun to watch then fallen asleep halfway through. As a result, she knew more about collecting evidence than about interpreting it.

As she brushed her teeth she thought about what little she knew. She and Seth had heard the single shot just as it was getting dark, when they were out walking. Seth had identified it as a rifle shot, and she believed him. Max had reacted strongly and run off in the direction of the sound, with Seth following, so he'd seen — or smelled — something. Seth had told her the night before that he hadn't seen or heard anyone in the woods, apart from the body. A woman, about her own age or slightly older. Not local, or Seth would probably have recognized her, since he'd grown up in Granford. What could have led her to that particular place? Or more likely, who? Seth had said there was no sign of a struggle: the woman had died from a single, well-placed rifle wound. She had fallen face-first and died. Or, for all Meg knew, she had died the moment the bullet entered her, or on the way down. Did it matter? She had died. More precisely, she had been murdered.

The shooter hadn't lingered to see if he'd done the job, but neither had he gone crashing off through the underbrush in a panic

— Seth would have heard him. So, no panic, just cold efficiency. But he had to have known someone would have heard the shot, and could easily have come out to investigate. Maybe. She wouldn't do it, but maybe a guy would. Seth had. Had the killer known that Seth was approaching?

Meg hoped fervently that Art had identified the woman and whoever had shot her, and they could close the case quickly. Then she could go back to worrying about earth-shaking things like how extensively she should prune her trees. She was grateful that the killer hadn't shot the poor woman in the orchard itself, because then it would be a crime scene — legally speaking in the near term, but in her mind, forever. Was there such a thing as a blood apple?

Meg shook her head to clear it. Not enough sleep, and now she had to go make lots of coffee for a bunch of already exhausted police officers. Did she have any coffee cake in the freezer? Why was she obsessing about food again? Was that what a traditional woman was supposed to do in times of crisis like this one? She tried to picture a man in her situation: would he start baking something as soon as he heard there was a body?

Seth stumbled down the stairs just as Art

pulled into the driveway, parked and headed for the kitchen door. Seth detoured around the table to let him in. Meg wondered idly if there were any women on the Granford police force. Maybe a woman would have more insight into what the dead woman was doing out there in the woods, and with whom. Somebody with a weapon, who killed her. Had the dead woman had any suspicion of what was to come?

"Good morning, Art. Coffee?"

"Thanks, Meg," Art said. "Hope it's strong — I haven't been home yet."

"You need eggs? Bacon? I'm happy to fix you breakfast, if it helps."

"Coffee first. Please."

Meg busied herself with cooking, while keeping her ears open. There wasn't much conversation going on, and why should there be? These policemen had been out all night in subfreezing weather and snow, looking for evidence in the dark to figure out who killed the unknown woman in their midst. "Have you called in the state guys yet?"

"Of course. I think they were waiting for daylight. Or maybe a helicopter, so they wouldn't get their boots wet. The guy I talked to kept asking, 'Are you sure it wasn't suicide?' Idiot. At least they trusted us to do the basic stuff. In the dark, with snow coming."

"You going to want my formal statement now?" Seth asked.

"Might as well get it since I'm here. After I've inhaled my first cup of coffee."

Meg handed him a full mug.

Before Art could start drinking it, he said, "Hey, Seth — you called me on your cell last night, right?"

"I did. It's become a habit, to keep it with me. You never know what you're going to run into."

"Please tell me you got some pictures before the snow started?" Art said plaintively.

Seth smiled. "Some, after I made sure she was dead. I'll send them to you. But I warn you, there wasn't much to see. I did the best I could, but it was dark. The woman was wearing dark clothes and was lying facedown. She had dark hair, not long. I found her in the midst of some scraggly woods with no distinguishing features. I didn't see a weapon anywhere nearby, but I didn't go looking for it — I figured someone would be mad if I trampled what little evidence there might be. Though I don't think there was much. Will the state police send their own forensic people?"

"Probably. Listen, let's get this statement over with. You don't mind if I record it?"

"Of course not."

"May I stay?" Meg asked.

"As long as you pretend you're not here. Or maybe we should start with you. Did you see or hear anything out of the ordinary last night?"

"Seth and I took a walk after dinner — we were going to look at the orchard, even though it was getting kind of dark. Mostly we just wanted some fresh air, and Max needed to go out anyway."

"Did you hear the gunshot?"

"Actually, we heard a couple of shots earlier in the afternoon, but they sounded farther away. Then a single one later. I asked Seth about them, since I didn't recall hearing shots around here last year. Oh, and I saw a fox go by, if that matters."

"Only if he's a witness. Does he live around here?"

"I have no idea," Meg told Art. "This is the first time I've noticed one."

"And you didn't see any other people during your walk?"

Meg shook her head. "Not a soul."

"Okay, that's all I've got for you. Seth, your turn. You told me you heard a shot that sounded pretty close. What did you do?"

"We had Max with us, and he took off toward the sound, so I followed."

"You weren't worried whoever it was might shoot at you?"

"It never occurred to me. Actually, I was more worried about Max and whether the shooter would think he was a deer, or some other animal that might attack."

"What did Max do?"

"I think the shooter was gone by the time Max reached the site, although I didn't hear him leave. Max would most likely have tried to make friends with him."

"Yeah, that's Max." Art sighed. "Do you know whether Max disturbed the body in any way?"

"Not that I could see."

"Describe the person you found."

"I didn't touch her. Before you ask, I could tell it was a woman from the start, even though she had heavy winter gear on."

"Tell me about that."

"Standard stuff. Heavy Carhartt coat, brown, not new. Jeans. Lace-up boots, also not new. Hat with earflaps, but they weren't down. Gloves."

"So nothing appeared out of place in the woods?"

"Nope. Not like she came from a party and was wearing heels and a sparkly dress.

Tell me, did you find any ID on her? Or a bag?"

Art shook his head. "No, nothing. Maybe she thought she was out for a stroll, or a romantic tryst, or even some late hunting, but she didn't have anything on her. Or in her pockets. I'm going to guess that whoever shot her took all that stuff with him."

"Or maybe she wasn't carrying anything. The timing is pretty tight. I didn't hear him leave, so when could he have cleaned out all her pockets? Or could he have done that before they set out?"

"It hadn't started snowing yet?"

"You mean, were there any footprints? No. It had just started when I called you."

Meg sat silently, listening to the semiformal conversation. Two friends, sitting in a warm kitchen, discussing death — for the permanent legal record. How odd it was.

"Art, has anyone been reported missing?" she asked suddenly.

"Nope, but it's still early. Could have been a guest. Could have been a hunter from somewhere else, staying at a local motel, or with a friend. Or even planning to drive home whenever she was finished doing . . . whatever she was doing. We may know more by the end of the day. I'd guess the state homicide cops will take a wider view, and they've got the resources to do it."

"You going to talk to my mother, Art?" Seth asked. "She might have heard or seen something."

"On my list, Seth." Art drained his mug and stood up. "I'd better keep moving or I'll fall asleep in a chair, or in my car. I'll get your statement typed up and let you know when you can stop by and sign it. Or heck, maybe you can do that online now — I don't keep up with all the bells and whistles."

"Whatever works for you, Art. Meg and I were kind of enjoying a little downtime, at least until last night, so we aren't exactly busy."

3

"Shoot, I forgot to tell Art to talk with the kids at my house. My former house. Whatever," Seth said, clearly annoyed at himself.

"Won't he think of that himself?" Meg asked.

"Maybe. But right now he's exhausted, and I'm not sure if he remembers I've rented it out or that anyone is living there."

"And you're wondering if there was someone at home, whether they heard anything?" Meg was struck by a chilling thought. "Or maybe it was one of them? Or a couple of them? And they happened to have a rifle and were fooling around in the woods and it went off?" That raised even more questions in Meg's mind. "Did you keep a gun at the house?"

"I've never owned a gun, Meg, although I know how to use one. I'd like to think I wouldn't be stupid enough to leave one there, knowing I'd be renting it out. Which of course doesn't take into account that somebody else in the family might have hidden one in the past and forgotten to tell me. But I can't imagine that anyone who owned that kind of weapon would leave it sitting around loaded."

"Do you know the names of the guys who are renting it, apart from Larry?"

"Not really. The others signed a basic lease, but I haven't memorized their names, and I haven't had any reason to drop in and talk with them. I guess I've been kind of relying on Larry to keep an eye on things — you know, make sure that the plumbing and heating work, that kind of thing. But at the same time, I don't think he's buddies with the other tenants, and they come and go pretty frequently. They're students. Maybe I'm just too trusting."

"That's not always a bad thing. And you must remember what it was like to be a college student, and what kind of job you did keeping a place reasonably livable. So, should we call Art and send him over there?"

"Art's most likely asleep right now, and he won't be happy if I wake him up to talk to a bunch of kids. Why don't you call? Larry's your employee."

"And he's your tenant!" Meg paused for a

moment and realized that they both seemed to be avoiding interrogating anyone, even if it was kindly meant. "I'm sorry. This is dumb. We've got only a few basic questions for him, or them." Meg started ticking them off on her fingers. "One, did he or anyone else hear anything suspicious last evening? Two, are any of the people living or staying at the house women? Not that I have any moral issues with that, but we need to know. Three, does anyone there have a rifle?" She sighed. "I need to talk to Larry anyway, and I don't think he has much of a social life so he's probably there now. I'll call his cell."

She punched in his cell number, but it rang and rang and finally went to voice mail. She left a brief message and shut off the app. "Not there," she told Seth. "You want to walk over and check things out? I'll come with you. For all I know, they've all been massacred and are lying in pools of blood. I've heard it's hard to get bloodstains out of old wood."

"Meg, sometimes you scare me. But we might as well check, and Max needs a walk anyway. Can we eat breakfast first?"

"I knew I was forgetting something. And remind me when we go that I should let the goats out, since it's a balmy twenty-five degrees."

"Sounds like a plan."

After a quick meal, they bundled up against the cold and went out the back door. Seth made sure he had Max's leash in one of his pockets. Meg greeted the goats and let them into the small field next to the barn, where they waited expectantly until she brought out more hay for them. "We won't be gone long, so don't worry."

"Do you always talk to the goats?" Seth asked, smiling.

"Sure. Shouldn't I? They always look so intelligent."

"Let me know when they start talking back."

They trudged up the hill, skirting the orchard. The night's storm clouds had disappeared and the sky was an intense blue; a cold breeze created small tornadoes of powdery snow that sparkled in the sun. It was exhilarating to be outside, breathing the cold clean air — as long as she didn't think about the body that had lain in the woods only a few hundred yards away. No sounds came from that direction, apart from a few birdcalls. Had the various police departments finished their investigations already? Or had the state police team decided to sleep in and arrive later? What snow there had been the night before would have obscured any sort of evidence. Now the sun was doing the work of melting it off, although the snow might linger in the shade of the trees.

It didn't take long to reach the house. Meg knew Seth kept a set of keys for it, but it seemed rude to barge in on whoever was inside, even though he had every right to. Instead he pounded on the front door, then pounded again. After a few minutes there was the sound of movement inside, and finally Larry pulled open the door, looking like he'd just crawled out of bed. "Hey, Larry," Meg greeted him. "You weren't answering your phone so we decided to come look for you."

"Oh. Uh. Is something wrong?"

"Yes, though I don't think it involves you. There was a shooting in the woods, over that way, on the other side of my house." Meg waved vaguely toward the stand of trees. "The police are investigating. Have they been here?"

"Nope, not that I know of. What happened?"

"That's what we're trying to figure out. Did you happen to hear a gunshot last night after dinner? Or see anybody lurking in the woods?"

Larry shook his head. "I had my headphones on — didn't hear a thing. And it was pretty dark by then."

"Are the rest of the tenants here?" Seth asked.

"I dunno," Larry said. "Like I told you, I had my headphones on. I was watching a movie. My door was shut."

Why was it almost everything that Larry said sounded evasive? Maybe it was an unconscious response — he'd grown up on a struggling farm, and managed to get himself a degree, but maybe it was intimidating to him to be surrounded by all these Amherst College eggheads. Or maybe she was being judgmental — maybe Larry really didn't care about chats on Eastern religions or renaissance painting over the dinner table, or maybe all the other occupants of the house were blue-collar workers and they all had a great time watching football or basketball or whatever.

"Mind if I go up and see if they're home?" Seth asked. "I'm not snooping, but this is a police investigation, and the more we find out, the better."

"Sure, go ahead. It's your place."

Seth went up the stairs and started knocking on doors. Larry seemed to be waking up gradually, and asked Meg, "Hey, you want some coffee or something?"

"Sure, fine. Kitchen?"

Larry nodded, then turned and made for the kitchen. Meg followed. The room was less of a pigsty than she had feared. Of course, she hadn't been inside a house occupied by young male students for quite a while, so she wasn't sure what current standards were. She cleared a space at the table — where last night's dishes were still scattered — and watched Larry boil water and spoon coffee into a pot. At least it wasn't instant.

"There are, what — three other guys living here? Since the beginning of the year?"

"Yeah, but I don't exactly know them. We all kind of keep to ourselves, you know?"

"I guess that makes it easier to get along."

Larry poured boiling water over the grounds. Seth came into the kitchen. "Nobody home," he said. "Did they not come home last night, or did they leave early?"

Larry shrugged. "I can't say. I don't keep track of them. You gonna tell me what this is all about?"

Seth sighed. "You'll hear soon enough. Like I said, someone was shot in those woods last night. Meg and I both heard the shot — we were out walking Max. Could've been hunters, although it was definitely too dark to see much. Anyway, Max took off to investigate, so I had to follow, and I found the body. Still bleeding a little, but definitely dead."

"Who was it?"

"I didn't know the person — it was a woman." Larry looked up then, startled, as Seth went on. "I called the local cops and they took over. Art Preston showed up quickly, and he said he called the state cops, but I don't know if they've done what they need to do yet."

"Anybody else know who it was?"

"So far, no. At least, Art didn't know earlier this morning, or if he did, he didn't share with us. He'd probably be the one they called first, since he was the first officer on the scene."

"Hunting accident?" Larry asked.

"No. The woman was shot in the back."

"Oh, wow. That's bad."

"You wouldn't know if any of your housemates had a woman visiting him?" Meg asked.

"I might have noticed that," Larry admitted.

"Meg, the woman was probably old enough to be these kids' mother," Seth pointed out. "Was somebody's mom visiting?"

"Not that I saw. So, you're saying somebody killed her? Out in the woods? Why?"

"Yes, she was killed. There's the location of the wound, for one thing. And she had no ID on her, although she could have left that wherever she was staying. She was dressed for the weather, at least, so she was probably out there deliberately, not because someone forced her. But there had to be someone else there. The one with the gun. Do you know how to handle a gun, Larry?"

"Sure. I grew up on a farm, remember? We were always shooting rats, maybe coyotes. But I've never hunted for food or sport. Just didn't care for killing things. And before you ask, I don't know if anybody else in the house owns a gun. I've never seen one here."

"My father had a shotgun," Seth said, "but that should still be at my mother's house. Meg, remind me to ask her if she's still got it."

"Are we going to go talk to her?"

"I suppose we should. She's probably too far from the scene to have heard anything, but I'd rather she found out about the death from me than from the police, or the news. She might have seen an unfamiliar car passing on the road. You don't have to come, you know."

"Of course I do," Meg protested. "I like

your mother. What's more, I know what it's like to be a woman living alone. No matter how careful you are, how many locks and sensors and what-have-yous you install, you still feel vulnerable. Maybe you men feel the same way but can't admit it, but women need to acknowledge those fears and have other people take them seriously. So I'm coming with you."

Seth looked sheepish now. "I'm sorry, to you and to all women I might have offended in the past. Apparently I'm an insensitive oaf. I would be happy to have you accompany me to my mother's house."

Larry had been watching this verbal ping-pong with bewilderment. "So should I be worried too?"

"I don't think so, unless you have reason to believe one of your current roommates is a killer."

"Only when he tries to cook," Larry muttered.

"Larry, we need to talk about pruning," Meg said, "but it can wait a day or two, unless you have other ideas. Otherwise, just keep your eyes open, and let someone know if you see something or someone odd. Have you seen any legitimate hunters on the property before now?"

Larry shook his head. "Not the best place

for deer, and not much else worth shooting these days. Anybody with half a brain would ask someone who knew the land where the best place to go would be." Meg and Seth exchanged a look: Larry agreed that a hunter would be out of place in this corner of Granford, particularly one accompanied by a woman. Or maybe both were hunters, out to prove something. In any case, the survivor had been careful to remove any obvious evidence, or had been counting on the snow to mess up the scene.

"You want to take Max?" Meg asked Seth.

"Either we walk from here and take Max or we take him back down the hill and drive over. Unless you want to dog-sit for a short time, Larry?"

"No problem. Max and me, we get along fine. And you and me, we need to talk about the tiny house idea. The weather should be getting better soon, and I'd like to get started before we get too busy in the orchard."

"Or you're getting fed up with dealing with a house full of roommates," Seth said, grinning at him. "Talk to me tomorrow and we'll make a plan. I'll collect Max after we've seen my mother. Oh, and if the police come to talk to you, just tell them what you told us."

"Got it. See you later."

4

Meg and Seth set out again. The temperature had warmed up a few degrees, and most of the snow was already gone.

"You really think my mother is afraid of being alone in her house?" Seth asked, puffing a bit as they continued up the hill.

"I said most women would be. Lydia is a sensible woman and not easily frightened. Does she own a gun?"

"No, or not that she's told me. But like I said, there used to be a shotgun at the house. Still, we never had any trouble at the house, the kind that required a gun."

"Seth, how many years have you lived in this part of town? The world has changed — haven't you noticed? High school kids have illegal guns now, and sometimes they use them."

"In Granford?"

"You tell me. You talk to Art more often that I do. But it's true in many places in the country, as far as that goes. Holyoke among them. Just because we've got pretty green trees and a white church on the green does not mean we're immune."

"Okay, point taken. You want me to get a gun, in case you need it when I'm not around?"

"No. Don't. I wouldn't use it. If I tried, I'd probably shoot myself in the foot, if I could remember where I'd hidden the cartridges." She grabbed Seth's coat sleeve. "I'm not saying this lightly, you know. I don't believe I could shoot another human being, even one who was threatening me."

"What if the person was threatening someone you cared about? A child? Me?"

"Seth, I'd rather not find out."

"And I hope you never will."

They'd reached Lydia's house, and Seth knocked at the kitchen door. Meg wasn't surprised when Christopher answered their knock: to anyone seeing him with Lydia, it was immediately obvious that they were very much a couple these days. "Come in, come in," Christopher said. "I suppose this isn't a social call."

"Not exactly," Seth admitted. "There was a shooting in the woods beyond our house last night. Someone died. I found the body not long after. I thought you should know, before someone else told you."

Lydia stood up quickly from her seat at the kitchen table and gave her son a hug. "Oh, Seth, how awful. Was it anyone we knew? Anyone local?"

"So far nobody knows, or at least as of the time we talked to Art Preston over breakfast. I'm sure he'll get around to talking to you, although I guess it's unlikely that you would have heard anything this far away, with your windows closed. But he'd been up all night, so he went home to get a few hours of sleep."

"Was it a hunting accident?" Christopher asked.

"No. Couldn't have been. The victim was shot in the back. There was no sign of the gun that killed her."

"Her?" Lydia said quickly, startled.

"Yes, it was a woman, about Meg's age. Dressed for the weather, but no ID on her. And no sign of the shooter. Art did the preliminary work, but he put in a call to the state police, after he'd checked to see if it was someone he knew from Granford. Of course, last night there was just enough snow to mess up anything like evidence."

"The person could have come from anywhere, no?"

Seth shrugged. "I don't know much. It

was dark and snowing, and when Art showed up at the scene I handed the whole thing over to him. Meg and I are just trying to help by talking to any people we know who might have heard or seen something. Which is itself a pretty short list."

"I would not want to undertake that investigation," Christopher said. "To the best of my knowledge, Amherst has a population of close to forty thousand people, and Northampton is close behind when the colleges are in session. A person or people could easily have come from either one, and from even farther afield as well. If the deceased was not known to the local authorities, it's a rather daunting task to find a single person. She could have been a student, a faculty member, a mere visitor, or someone just passing through. No sign of a vehicle, I presume?"

"Not that I know of. Let me get the official part of my visit over with, if I can call it that — I'm just trying to help out Art. Did you hear a gunshot around seven o'clock last night? It would have been a rifle, not a handgun." Lydia and Christopher exchanged a glance, and Lydia answered for them both. "No. As you said, the windows were all closed, and we were watching a movie at the other end of the house."

Seth went on, "Have you seen any strangers roaming around lately? Singly or a pair? Anybody acting suspicious? Anybody carrying a rifle, with or without a case?"

This time Christopher spoke. "I think I can safely say that the answer to all of those questions is no. We have the advantage of a clear view in all directions from this house, and movement is apt to catch my eye, as well as Lydia's. That means that we must entertain the possibility that this unfortunate death was planned in advance, and the killer sought to leave as little evidence as possible behind, and sought to avoid detection. And apparently he — or she — is a fair shot, since there was only the one report. But he did not think through his plan adequately. Perhaps he was not from this part of the state? Surely he would have been aware that domestic animals wander through the area? The body could have been found far sooner than he would have liked."

"That's one possibility," Seth agreed. "But what if he had planned to remove the body but was interrupted? Maybe even by Meg and me? I'm sure anyone could hear us coming for miles on a still night. And then there was Max."

"Seth, are you saying we were that close to walking in on the murder, or right after?"

Meg asked anxiously.

"Oh, my dear, perhaps I should not have suggested that," Christopher said, sounding contrite. "Surely this is a safe place to walk, or to exercise your dog."

"Somehow it doesn't feel quite as safe as it seemed yesterday," Meg said softly.

"Have you had breakfast? Or would you like some coffee?" Lydia asked, and Meg wondered if she was trying to change the subject.

"Thanks, Mom," Seth said, "but Meg and I ate early. We were going to go over some plans, and I want to talk to Larry about the space we're building for him so we can get started as soon as it warms up enough. I get the feeling he doesn't enjoy having a batch of roommates, even if the price is right. Which is to say, nothing."

"I suppose I can understand that, dear. You'll let us know if Art finds out anything new?"

"Of course."

Meg was already pulling on her coat. "Lydia, you and I really should get together, while we both have time. I've got a lot of thinning to do in the orchard, but I've been waiting for Larry to give me the go-ahead. I'm still afraid of doing more harm than good."

"I understand. But please, be careful! Both of you."

When Meg and Seth had gotten beyond earshot, Meg said, "I feel badly that we had to upset Lydia, although I understand your reasons for telling her first."

"This whole thing has been upsetting, all the more so because we don't know who did it. You know I've lived here all my life, and I've always felt secure here. Heck, half the time my father didn't even lock up the plumbing supplies for the business. We knew our neighbors and trusted them. There simply weren't many strangers roaming around, even in hunting season."

"But what about the colleges? There were always new people coming and going there."

"Yes, but mainly students and faculty focused on their classes or getting a degree. Sometimes they'd cut loose and get drunk on a weekend, but that was the exception, not the rule. And fewer kids had cars when I was their age, so they couldn't roam around getting into trouble. Besides, this doesn't feel like a prank gone wrong or an accident. Somebody wanted that woman dead."

They both fell silent as they made a detour to Seth's house to retrieve Max. When Larry handed him over, Seth said, "Can the tiny house plans wait until tomorrow?"

"No problem," Larry replied. "See you then."

When they were back at their house, Seth held the door open for them. Once inside he said, "Is your computer on the dining room table?"

"Yes. Why?"

"There's something I want to check."

"Okay," Meg said, slightly mystified. "You want any more coffee?"

"Sure, fine." Clearly Seth's mind was somewhere else as he sat down at the table and turned on the laptop. By the time the coffee was ready, he returned to the kitchen, triumphantly brandishing a color printout of something. "You need to take a look at this," he said.

"Okay. What am I looking at?" Meg asked, setting a mug of coffee in front of Seth and pulling up a chair next to him.

"This is an aerial photo of our properties. Take a minute so you can figure out where we are."

It took her a couple of moments to orient herself, and then things kind of clicked. "Okay, I see it. Here's my house" — she laid a finger on a length of road with a row of houses along it — "and here's yours and your mother's. Right?"

"Exactly."

"I don't know why I never looked at this view before, or not carefully. I've seen all the old maps, the first ones that show our properties. There are quite a few more houses now, aren't there?"

"There are, and as I said earlier, fewer farms. But the road has been here since the eighteenth century. There's a document at the town hall in Northampton that describes laying out the road, with directions like 'turn left at Widow Smith's barn,' or 'go fifty rods past the old oak.' It's fun to read, although I'd guess most of those landmarks are long gone."

"There's the field behind this place." Meg pointed to a squarish open plot on the map. "What was it you wanted me to see?"

"Look beyond the field, to the east. It's all wooded, for at least a mile."

Meg could see a swath of green at the end of her property. "But part of that is boggy, at least when there's a wet spring or summer. Why does this matter?"

"Because the trees run all the way down to the road, and quite a ways to the north. I'd guess they follow the brook, which was too wet to develop, like you said. But my point is that someone could park down the road from here and enter the woods, and no one would see him — or them — coming or going. He might need to know about the boggy patches, but that wouldn't be hard to figure out. Would you say that the shot could have come from the east of where we were walking?"

"It's possible. I wasn't really paying attention, but I'm pretty sure it came from the woods. Which means the shooter didn't have to live around here, just know enough about the land to make his way through it without getting stuck in the mud. Although the ground is pretty well frozen this time of year, so even that wouldn't be a problem. Is that what you're trying to say?"

"I suppose. I don't want to believe that we're in danger from any of our neighbors, or that anyone else nearby is. Maybe I'm playing ostrich with its head in the sand, but I'd rather think that the killer came from somewhere else and chose this place because he knew it but nobody here knew him. Am I making any sense?"

"I think so. In any case, I love it that you're trying to protect your tribe here, or at least make us *feel* protected."

"That's what we cavemen do."

Meg couldn't resist smiling as she tried to picture Seth as a caveman. "Did Art say he was coming back, or did he have other people to talk to?"

"I can give him a call," Seth said, "and he can decide whether he wants to talk to our neighbors or settle for my secondhand report. Or maybe the state police have taken it out of his hands anyway, and we can expect a visit from them sometime. But let's let Art get a couple of hours of sleep first."

"Good idea. We're not exactly officially involved anyway, right? Just innocent by-standers?"

"Unless you count that I found the body, and I certainly know the lay of the land in this part of town. Maybe I could sign on as a consultant."

"I'll let you figure that out. Me, I have no standing here, and no experience with weapons or forensics." Except, she reflected, that she'd encountered her share of bodies since she'd arrived in Granford.

5

Meg and Seth armed themselves with more coffee, then settled at the kitchen table again.

"I never thought I'd dislike having free time," Meg said, "but I'm feeling kind of twitchy. There's nothing I have to do in the orchard right this moment, although I'm sure Larry will give me a long list of tasks any day now. We've seen your mother, although I wouldn't call it a social visit, exactly. But she already had, um, company anyway. Where do you think she and Christopher are heading?"

Seth smiled. "This is my mother, remember. Are you asking if she and Christopher are likely to get married? Cohabit, or whatever it's called these days? Or will they muddle along simply enjoying each other's company when the spirit moves them?"

"Seth Chapin, I swear you're blushing!" Meg told him, laughing. "How do you feel about all or any of those options?"

"Bottom line is, I want my mother to be happy. She didn't have an easy life with my father, and I think after he passed away she enjoyed her freedom, up to a point. But then my marriage broke up — and I don't think she ever really warmed up to my ex, Nancy — and there was the problem with my brother. And I guess it could be lonely up there in a house meant for a family, and filled with memories."

"But, Seth, what do you think would be best for her? Or for both of them?"

"She's a grown woman. If she wants to marry Christopher, I'm all for it. He's a great guy — smart, interesting — and he really seems to care for her. I think they're both of a generation that would stick to the conventional rules, so I assume that means marriage. With my blessing, and with Rachel's too, I'm guessing. You okay with that?"

"Of course I am. I like Lydia. I'd like her even if she wasn't your mother. And of course I like Christopher. Without his help I wouldn't be sitting here now, with you, and for that I'll always be grateful."

"Well, I'm glad that's settled," Seth said. "Shall we tell them or let them figure it out for themselves?"

Meg smiled. "I think they can handle it. I wouldn't worry about them. So, now that we've taken care of their lives, what are we doing today? It's too cold for outdoor house chores. Anything need doing inside the house?"

"I'd rather not tear things up when it's still this cold. And if you wanted to paint or varnish something, you'd have to open the windows."

Meg stifled a laugh. "Have you seen *Camelot*? King Arthur and Guinevere share a song, 'What Do the Simple Folk Do?' which fits us pretty well right now. We don't know what to do with ourselves when we're not crazy busy." When she heard a car pull into the driveway and stop, followed by another, she added, "Maybe we're about to get busier."

Seth stood and went to the back door and waited to open it. "Looks like Art and — damn, Detective Marcus."

"Well, we knew he'd be involved at some point, didn't we? I'll boil some more water for coffee. Remind me later to make a couple of batches of cookies to freeze for occasions like this."

Seth opened the door to Art and Detective William Marcus. Neither man looked happy, so this had to be an official call, Meg surmised. Seth nodded at the two men and gestured them toward the kitchen table. "This okay? We can sit in the dining room if you need more space."

"Seth, Meg," Detective Marcus said perfunctorily. Apparently their relationship had not warmed up yet, Meg thought with some regret. "I hope this won't take long — the kitchen is fine."

"Coffee?" Meg asked, feeling like a waitress. Surely she'd earned a seat at the table by now, but she always had the feeling that Marcus didn't approve of her participation — even though it had produced results in his cases more than once.

"No, thanks," Marcus said. Art just shook his head.

When everyone was seated, Marcus took the lead. "I have some information about the woman whose body you found, Seth. Please do not repeat this to anyone outside this room, at least for the moment. Her name was Jenn Chambers, and she worked for the *Boston Globe* as a freelancer. She was doing research on current drug problems in the Pioneer Valley for an article she hoped to write. She intended it to be a substantial piece, and she was investigating all aspects, including what drugs came in and how, how they were distributed, the importance of the drug trade in both the college and rural communities in particular, and so on. To avoid any misunderstandings, she talked to the state police first to alert us to her presence, and she agreed to share what information she collected before publication, although in exchange we agreed not to censor what she wrote as long as it didn't endanger anyone. And she promised to give us a heads-up when it was going to run. She was a respected journalist, but her face was not well known, so she felt comfortable working on her own and posing as a newcomer to the community. Apparently someone saw through that, and that's why she died. Or so we believe."

"She talked to you before she started investigating?" Meg asked.

"No. She actually approached the narcotics unit first, since that was her primary interest. That unit alerted me to her presence and asked that I give her free rein. Of course, following her death I had to become involved, but the narcotics unit asked that I not release any details."

"Interesting. You've officially dismissed the idea of a hunting accident?" Seth said carefully.

"Art has given me your interview and filled me in on your comments. Based on the absence of any physical evidence, yes, I have eliminated that as an option. But much as I hate to admit it, there is little more to go on at this time. Given the narcotics unit's reaction to the news, I think we have to assume her death was drug-related, but I am not directly involved in that aspect of law enforcement, nor would Art be."

Seth nodded. "I see. I think. Of course Meg and I have been discussing this, and based on the topography of our properties, we wondered if it was possible that the woman was shot elsewhere and dumped here. If you look at an aerial photograph, you can see there's a route through the adjacent woods that would conceal that kind of activity."

"You said you heard the shot," Marcus said neutrally, without commenting on Seth's suggestions.

"Yes. Or I should say, we both heard a shot coming from the woods, and when I found the body the blood was still wet. But even so, it could have been a deliberate diversion. Did your people find much blood at the scene?"

"Possibly enough to support either scenario," Marcus admitted reluctantly. "We have not located any vehicle that could have brought her or her shooter here. It is also possible that the meeting was prearranged and the killer chose this as an isolated location with few potential observers."

"Where was she staying?" Meg asked.

"We don't know yet. Nor have we found her car, assuming she had one."

"So the killer brought her here, before or after she was shot. Does that suggest that he knew this area? Or even lives nearby?"

"We have not eliminated that."

Meg wondered what it would take to loosen the man up. Maybe she should spill a cup of hot coffee in his lap.

"Have you found anyone who saw anything out of the ordinary?" Seth asked.

"You're thinking of your neighbors? No, nobody reported anything unusual. It was a cold night, and most people were at home watching some form of entertainment. And as you no doubt know, gunshots are not particularly rare at this time of year."

"*Is* there a drug problem in Granford, Detective?" Meg asked.

"Compared to other local communities, it is relatively minor, but it exists everywhere these days, sad to say, and it's growing. There has been a startling increase of opioid arrests and medical crises in the Pioneer Valley over the past two to three years, and that's what this reporter was looking at. Why the surge now, why this area?"

Meg looked at Seth. "I feel like I should apologize for being so uninformed. Seth, has this come up in Town Meetings?"

Seth shook his head. "Not in any detail. That doesn't mean it doesn't exist around here. We'd like to think Granford is a bubble of innocence compared to the surrounding communities, but that's probably naïve. But I will say that strangers tend to stand out around here. It's not like we're a tourist destination."

"You might be surprised, Seth," Art finally spoke up. "Drug dealers aren't all shady characters with black hoodies skulking in corners. It could be a schoolteacher who's having trouble making ends meet and sees dealing as a quick solution. If he's careful he — or she — could get away with it. Of course, kids have a way of finding things out."

"Have you talked to the high school students?" Meg asked.

"Not yet," Art admitted. "Detective Marcus here doesn't want to attract any attention to this investigation until we have to. What kids can overhear, they can also let slip to the wrong people."

"I see." Meg turned back to Detective Marcus. "Why are you telling us this, Detective?" she asked. "Apart from the fact that Seth found Jenn's body and it was on one of our properties, or the next-door neighbor's. I appreciate you filling us in, but what are we supposed to do about it? Logically, if there is drug activity going on around here, wouldn't the dealers lay low for a while, until the murder investigation is over?"

"It's possible. There are a lot of factors involved. Or perhaps the dealers think everyone in Granford is an oblivious hick who wouldn't recognize that kind of illegal activity even if it was happening in the supermarket checkout line in front of them." Detective Marcus held up a hand before Meg could protest. "I'm not saying it's true, but it may be what those dealers believe. They may have a lot of money at stake. Or maybe not. There's a lot we don't know."

"I appreciate that you've told us, Detective," Seth said, "but as Meg asked, what are we supposed to do with this information?"

"Keep your eyes and ears open. When you hold a town meeting, you can raise the general issue of drug problems in your town, without giving any specifics. I wouldn't go so far as to call a special meeting, because that would tip our hand. Give us some time to investigate. Otherwise, go on about your business. I'm sure we all hope this will be cleared up quickly."

"Of course," Meg said. Seth nodded his agreement.

The detective stood up. "If you hear or see anything suspicious, please contact us. But don't run around playing amateur detective — that could do more harm than good. I'll see myself out."

As Detective Marcus walked out of the kitchen and out to his car, Art showed no signs of moving. Finally he said, "First, let me apologize for not filling you in sooner. Last night, in the dark and the snow, I didn't recognize the woman, and as you know, I called Homicide at once. When I got hold of Marcus, he shut me down, told me not to talk about who she might be, and he admitted that order came from the narcotics unit. I don't think investigating drug dealing is exactly his strong suit — he's homicide. But reading between the lines, I think narcotics has a plan of their own, and they don't want Marcus or any of us tramping through it."

"So Marcus doesn't know what to do next?" Meg asked. "Who's taking the lead?"

"That remains to be seen. Okay, spill it, you guys. I'm sure you've already talked to your closest neighbors, a fact you didn't bother to mention to Marcus."

"You know us too well, Art," Seth said. "I told my mother and Christopher, because they're bound to hear it somewhere and it seemed only fair, in the event they might be at risk. I also asked Larry if he had heard anything, but he said he had his headphones on while watching a movie and wasn't paying attention."

"He's living up in your house, right?" Art asked.

"Until we build him his own."

"Oh, right, I think you mentioned that. You're converting the old chicken house, right?"

"Yup."

"That's either a brilliant idea or the stupidest thing I've heard for a while," Art told him.

"Let's just say he values his privacy, and he isn't into material things. Someplace warm and dry with indoor plumbing will suit him fine, or so he says."

"Of course, it could make a great playhouse for kids, down the line. Nothing you want to share?" Art cocked one eyebrow at Meg.

"Art, we've been married about fifteen minutes," Meg told him. "Give us some time, will you? I promise, if there's anything to report, you'll be the first to know — after our mothers, of course." She paused before adding, "You really haven't heard anything about drugs around here?"

"Rumors of kids smoking pot is about the worst I've heard. I'll admit I'm out of my depth as much as Marcus. The world is changing too fast for me, or maybe I'm just getting old." He stood up. "I'd better get to work, dealing with the important stuff like parking violations and littering. Now those I understand."

"I'll walk you out," Seth volunteered.

When the men had left, Meg continued to sit at the table, drinking her now-cool coffee and staring into space. She knew that Art's question about having kids was probably on the whole town's mind — most people knew Seth and liked him. So of course they'd be curious, and they meant well. But she and Seth hadn't really discussed it — yet. She'd always thought he'd make a great father, but she wasn't so sure about whether she was suited to be a mother. Her life had changed so much in the past two years, and she was still trying to settle into her new life. She had so much to learn about raising apples and running a small business! Where would a baby fit? Did she want to find out? And how long could she wait before deciding?

6

When Seth finally came back, Meg was still sitting where he'd left her. She could have called it thinking, but maybe it was more like avoiding thinking. It always amazed her that one small event could alter the course of a life — or end it. One minute a presumably talented, experienced newspaper reporter was deep into a timely and challenging investigation, and the next she was dead from a single bullet. That fact was testimony to how important her chosen subject was — if it was worth killing for — but it was also a tragic waste that such a person should be silenced. Clearly it was important to a lot of people that this murder be solved, but she wished it hadn't happened. Some small part of Meg mourned the loss of innocence — the sense that Granford was somehow immune to the dangers that the rest of the world faced. But where would she rather be? The good citizens of Granford were engaged in their community — witness Seth's participation in the Town Council, despite the demands of his own business — and hardworking and decent. Which might have made the town a good place for drug dealers and killers to lay low, because no one expected to see them in such an idyllic setting.

Seth stopped to study her expression as he approached. "You look . . . I don't know what. Depressed? Sad?"

"I guess I am. I wanted to believe that Granford was a safe good place to live, to plan a life, but now I wonder if I was wearing rose-colored glasses all along. I mean, I'm an optimist. I lose my job and the fates, by way of my mother, hand me a working farm that included a place to live and a profession that challenges me. I mean, I've got a good education and a good professional track record — there were plenty of other things I could have done. I even planned to do them — you know, polished up my résumé, put together a list of people to network with. Yet here I am. Please don't take this wrong, but you — falling in love with you and marrying you — had nothing to do with my being here, although it gave me another reason to stay. But the primary reason was that I chose to play out the hand

I'd been dealt and see what happened. You're part of the 'what happened.' "

"This murder has really shaken you up, hasn't it." It was a statement, not a question. "Which *Star Wars* movie was it where somebody said they felt a great disturbance in the Force? Not that Granford has reached quite that cosmic scale, but a violent killing of a stranger within our boundaries is profoundly disturbing to all of us who choose to live here. It does make us question our assumptions. But where else would you go? Where are things better?" He sat down next to Meg and took her hand in his.

"I'm sorry. Now I'm depressing you too. So what's the solution?"

"We try to fix it."

"You mean try to solve the murder and prove that it was a fluke rather than the result of a creeping sickness in our town? That always makes Detective Marcus *soooo* happy with us."

"He's a good man, even if he kind of lacks empathy. And from what I've heard, he's a good police officer. But we have an advantage: we're insiders. We know the town and its people, not just casually but from long experience. People here have roots that go back a long way. Even you do — as you

71

know, you wouldn't be here if some distant relative hadn't left the place to your mother. That's a personal connection, even if you don't know all the details."

"You aren't going to go all woo-woo on me now, are you, Seth? The ancestors called me home?" Meg asked, finally managing to produce a smile.

"What, that your ancestors brought you here for a purpose? No, I won't go that far. But tell me you don't feel some sort of commitment to this place, this town, and you want to see things made right. And that means figuring out who killed Jenn, if we can."

"Bypassing the police?"

"No, contributing what we know or find out, that they can't. Partnering. We're smart enough to keep out of their way if need be, but we do possess some advantages. Like insider knowledge. Not of drugs, but of people here."

Meg felt a flicker of hope. "Okay, I'm in. Where do we start?"

"We already have. We showed Detective Marcus the lay of the land with that aerial photo. He might not have thought to look at that particular view on his own."

"He might also tell us we're trying to make it look like the killer came from somewhere outside Granford, for our own reasons."

"Maybe. But turn that around: based on what we know about Granford, we don't believe the killer came from here, so we're looking for an alternative explanation. And we found a possible one, that he chose Granford because it was a good place to hide out. Or so he thought."

"I still say he scouted the location ahead of time. He couldn't have been that lucky, to stumble over it," Meg protested.

"Say he did. Say he made a conscious decision to find a place that had nothing to do with him, that provided some cover, where a passing stranger, even one with a rifle, wouldn't look unusual if he went tramping through the woods."

"Does that make the search easier or harder?"

"I can't say, but at least it offers another option."

"All right, Sherlock, what do we do next?"

"I don't have a clue. Oh, sorry — bad pun. You know, if this hadn't happened literally in our backyard, I might have stayed blissfully ignorant of the whole drug problem, and that troubles me. I'm an elected town councilman, so I should be aware of issues like this, or else I should give up the position and let the town find someone else who is more on top of things."

"Well, from my perspective, I dislike those books where some ditzy young woman decides she's smarter than the local police and sets off to solve crimes, usually putting herself, her loved ones and her friends at risk. That's not an intelligent way to do things. Marcus doesn't like amateurs meddling in his business, and I can understand that. But you and I didn't start out to meddle — we were forced into this by the killer. I would like to be able to find a way to collaborate with the police, to give them information that we have better access to than they do without stepping all over their toes. Is that possible, do you think?"

"In a perfect world, maybe." Seth stood up and started pacing around the kitchen. "No, that sounds cynical. We just have to find a way to convince Detective Marcus that we'd be an asset rather than a nuisance so that he'd actually listen to us, and then stay out of his way."

"Not an easy task," Meg said. "Seth, are you sure this is a good idea? I know we can contribute, but he seems to be locking horns with the narcotics unit over what Marcus sees as his jurisdiction — homicide — and to come trotting to him with our little bits of evidence is kind of like rubbing salt into his wounds, isn't it? He's been told he can't act on it. Anyway, he seems to glare at me every time he sees me. And if he's wrestling with the narcotics unit over jurisdiction, that's only going to get worse." Meg stopped for a moment to think. "You know, we might enlist Christopher in this."

"Why?" Seth asked.

"Because he's a college professor with lots of students, some of whom know a lot about chemistry." When Seth started to protest, Meg held up a hand. "Hear me out. I know he seems a bit unworldly, but he does see a lot of younger people on a day-to-day basis, so he might notice some unusual behavior, especially if he's looking for it."

"You mean caused by drugs? And what would unusual behavior look like?" Seth asked with a half smile.

"I only know what I see on television or in movies, but I think you can guess. People looking for dark corners where they swap cash for a plastic bag of something-or-other. I'm going to make the assumption that they aren't using credit cards for their transactions. Or what about students who either nod off in class or suddenly become uncharacteristically hyperactive?"

"Interesting, but there are plenty of other

explanations for that kind of behavior, starting with lack of sleep or, at the other end, too much caffeine."

"But Christopher is a scientist. He should be able to distinguish, and he has plenty of time to observe. Look, I'm trying to be helpful here. I won't claim that he's going to make the bust of the decade in his class, but he might make a note of nontypical behavior."

"I guess it's worth talking to him about," Seth admitted.

"Your enthusiasm is overwhelming. Okay, you come up with an idea."

"I'm coming up blank."

"Let me ask you one thing, then," Meg pressed. "Did you, in your misspent youth, ever try any illicit substances?"

"Uh, no comment."

"I'll take that as a yes of sorts. I was more or less the same. I thought I should try a thing or two, just to see what everyone was talking about, but none of them ever appealed to me. They made me either stupid or nauseous, neither of which I enjoyed. I've stuck to wine ever since, and you must have noticed by now that a glass or two puts me to sleep."

Seth smiled at her. "Listen to us — we've turned into our parents. My dad's drink of choice was whiskey, and my mom drank only on Christmas and her birthday, and even then not much. But on a more serious note, the variety and effects of contemporary drugs are much broader and more complex, and the symptoms are harder to detect or interpret. And I'm sure the prices for buyers are all over the map. Of course, college kids have a lot more disposable cash these days than I ever did when I was their age."

"The world has changed around us. So where are we?"

"Still thinking, if you ask me. And it's been less than twenty-four hours since the poor woman died, and the news hasn't even gone public yet. Maybe Detective Marcus will wrap the case up before sundown."

"We can only hope."

As she got up to wash their few dishes, Meg realized that while it had been an interesting and thought-provoking discussion, they'd backed away from any mention of babies. Was that deliberate? Or maybe she needed to look at the broader picture: Did she want to bring a child into this increasingly unstable world? Would global warming destroy her apple trees within the next few years? Or would widespread colony collapse disorder eliminate so many bees that there would be none left to pollinate her orchard, even if the trees survived? Of course, if that turned out to be true, a lot of other people would be suffering as well, since plants that required pollination would dwindle. So where did a child fit?

Maybe it was time to get together with Seth's sister Rachel, whose youngest child, Maggie, was a few months old now, and study the real thing. Rachel had been very discreet about bringing up the issue when they were all together. Or maybe she just figured that she'd done her part for the family by producing three grandkids for Lydia and that was enough. She didn't feel any need to nag Meg to add to the population.

"Seth?" she said. When he looked up, she went on, "Why don't we have all your family over for a big dinner, since we've got time on our hands? I like winter cooking — I can make nice slow stews, and I could bake a cake — you know, make things I never have time for during apple season. And I haven't seen Rachel and her gang for a while."

"Sounds nice," Seth said. "When?"

"Let's try for tomorrow — that gives me time to get some food in and clean up the place," Meg told him. And maybe the combined police forces would have solved the murder by then. Maybe.

7

Larry showed up at the back door in the early afternoon. When Meg opened the door, he asked, "Is Seth here?"

"Sure is. Were you two going to talk about the tiny house?"

"I think so — he said he wanted to."

"Come on in," Meg said, stepping back to let him pass. "Have you eaten? Or do you want something to drink?"

"Nah, I'm good. Hi, Seth."

"Larry! Just the person I wanted to see."

"What?" Larry asked, looking startled by Seth's enthusiasm.

"We've got free time at the moment, and I thought we could use it to get the tiny house started. Or even finished by the time you and Meg have to get to work in the orchard, if we move fast. You're still interested, right? Because I'm okay with it if you want to stay in the other house. This was just an idea."

"No, I like the idea of a place of my own,

and I don't care if it's small. The house is kind of noisy. I mean, it's normal noise, but I'm not used to it."

"Did you ever live in a dorm when you went to college, Larry?" Meg asked.

"No, I lived at home and took classes. Couldn't afford the extra fees. Why?"

"So you've never had the experience of living in a building with a couple of hundred college boys. I hear they're kind of rowdy, not that I'd know from personal experience. Women's dorms are quieter. I've always heard a lot of the guys in dorms ended up flunking out, often in their first year, at least at the universities with large student populations, because they spend more time partying than studying."

"I wouldn't know. Seth, we don't need to do this if it's too much work."

But Seth wouldn't be diverted, Meg noted. "I want to. I like the idea, and it sounds like fun. We've already got a foundation in place, and I think we should either use it or tear it down, and I hate to waste anything that's already built. It looks like it's been there a long time. But if you're going to be the first occupant, I thought you should have some say in what goes into it. Don't worry — this is just talk. I've never actually seen one, but there's plenty of

81

information on the internet. Come on, sit down — we're just spit-balling here. Meg, you joining us?"

"Maybe. I was thinking about baking some cookies while you guys make plans, since people seem to keep dropping in on us. But I think a woman's opinion might be useful in figuring out how a small space would be most efficient to live in."

"I won't argue with that. Maybe we should work on the dining room table — it's larger. And the computer is there. Let me go dig up some paper and lined pads and we can get started."

When Seth left to find some materials, Meg said, "Larry, don't feel you have to go along with this if you don't want to. I think Seth is going a little stir-crazy, since there's not much construction or renovation going on at the moment and he doesn't know what to do with himself. On the other hand, if you work together you might be able to finish this quickly, and he'd feel good about having completed something. Maybe after you two figure out whatever plans you need, then we can talk about what needs to be done in the orchard."

"I'm cool with it, and I don't mind doing the work. I spent a lot of time back on our farm just trying to keep things together and running, so I know how things work, and I can use most tools. I can pull my own weight."

"Hey, guys," Seth called out from the next room. "You coming?"

Meg and Larry trooped dutifully into the dining room and settled themselves around the table, with Seth at the head. He started explaining quickly. "We know the existing foundation is about twenty by twenty-five feet, outside dimensions, and I don't want to rebuild it. We might need to shore it up a bit, but I think it's fundamentally sound, and the footings are deep enough to support the weight. They built things to last in the old days, even chicken coops, and I guess they had plenty of stone to work with. So that's the size we're starting with. Off the top of your head, what do you want inside, Larry?"

Larry looked startled at being questioned directly. "Well, uh, the obvious, I guess. Running water, heat, light. Someplace to cook and a space to sleep. That's about it."

"One or two levels? I mean, do you want a loft above for sleeping? That'd give you more floor space downstairs."

"Sure, okay. I can handle getting in and out of a loft. And the heat'll rise in winter so it will stay warm."

"Good point. Now, about utilities, we kicked around some ideas back in January, but there are practical issues to think about. If we want to run power lines, we have to involve the town and get permits. Not impossible, but it might slow things down. Now, for heat —"

Larry interrupted him. "Propane is easy to install, and economical. Or maybe a wood-burning stove — there's plenty of deadwood coming from the orchard and the surrounding woods to feed it. Or maybe even both."

"Right — plus you could use the propane to cook, if you needed to. Then there's water."

"You have a well here?" Larry asked.

"For the house, yes, although there's municipal water out on the street. You planning to bathe a lot?" Seth asked.

"What? Oh, are you joking? Sometimes, anyway. How do you calculate how much water you need?"

"I'd have to look that up. There might be a tipping point between tapping into the original wellhead versus the cost of drilling a new small one closer to the tiny house. Town water would cost us some money, plus running a line from the road to the back. Oh, and when it comes to laying out the inside, it makes sense to keep all the plumbing concentrated in one area — you know, sink, toilet, kitchen." Seth was busy scribbling notes as he spoke. "Now, back to power."

"What're the choices?"

"What're you going to be using inside there?" Seth countered. "Television? Music devices? Computer and printer? Anything else? At the very least you'll have to charge your cell phone. And, of course, some lights. The cook-stove can run on propane, as you pointed out."

"Will the town approve an extra electric line?"

"Maybe. Probably. But it won't come cheap."

"I don't want to cost you money. What about a gas-powered generator?"

"We could do that, but you'd have to be responsible about keeping it running. I think the power line is a better long-term prospect. We could put the wiring in place, and then use the generator for a while and see how it goes. If it's not enough, it can be replaced in the future." Seth added more scribbles to the large pad in front of him. "Look, we don't have to decide all this today — I'm just laying out the choices we need to make before we start construction.

Anything else you can think of now?"

"I know I walk by the place, like, every day, but is it open on all sides? With windows?"

"What do you mean?" Seth asked.

"Well, it's not in the middle of a stand of trees, right? Or does it have bushes around it?"

"You're worried about feeling exposed," Meg said suddenly. "We can certainly put up curtains."

"It's not just that — it's kinda like being unprotected. But that's good in a way, because nobody can sneak up on you."

"Are you worried about that, Larry?" Meg asked softly.

Larry looked down at his hands in his lap. "Sometimes, maybe. The place where I grew up, it was really out in the country, more than here. There were other animals around — lots of deer, coyotes, once even a bear. Funny how much noise animals can make at night, when there aren't other sounds like cars to cover it up."

"Larry, you don't have to do this if you'd rather be around more people," Seth said. "Just because I'm getting carried away with the idea doesn't mean you have to like it."

"It's okay, really. I have to get used to it. Heck, I grew up with quiet nights and animals. It'll be fine. Anything else we need to decide?"

"Why don't you go online and look at pictures of some examples of this kind of thing?" Seth suggested. "You might get some ideas about layouts and size."

"Yeah, sure, good idea. When were you thinking of starting, Seth?"

"I'll need to put some measurements together and then get the materials. Later this week, maybe, weather permitting? But we'll need to decide on the utilities first. Why don't you sleep on it and we can talk in the morning?"

"Sounds good. If you don't need me for anything else right now, I'd better be going. Meg, maybe we can talk about pruning tomorrow?"

"Works for me, Larry."

Larry left without any further comment. "He's still a little rough around the edges, isn't he?" Seth commented.

"He's worked hard to get where he is, and he does know how to manage an orchard — Christopher vouches for him. Socially he's a bit awkward, but he's young. He seemed very nervous about something, though. You think he really likes the idea of a tiny house or he's just trying to please you?"

"He doesn't work for me, he works for

you," Seth replied. "I thought he was into the whole idea, when we first talked about it. Maybe this shooting has him spooked?"

"I can't imagine why. He was raised in the country, so he must be used to the sound of gunshots, and using guns. Maybe he's just confused about the idea. He thinks he should want to have a space of his own, but maybe he grew up with five brothers sharing one room and he's never been really alone. I don't know much about his history and personal life, and I certainly don't know him well enough to get psychological with him. As you said, he's my employee. Maybe you can get something out of him when you start building."

"Hey, I don't want the burden of this to fall on him. It's a long-term investment. It gives us a little extra living space — not to mention privacy — if someone wants it. If it doesn't work out, we simply convert it into storage, or make it into a playhouse for Rachel's kids. It won't be expensive, except maybe for setting up the utilities."

"Seth, you're acting like a kid with a new toy, but I agree with your reasons. One question, though — will you go ahead with it if Larry scrapes up the courage to tell you he's not interested?"

"Hey, am I really being that pushy?"

Meg laughed. "I'm not going to get in the middle of that argument — and I don't think you know what it means to be obnoxiously pushy. But you do seem to think your enthusiasm should be contagious."

"Fine, I won't push Larry, but I still want to go ahead. I think I told you a while back, I can use it as a sample for potential customers, so they can see what kind of work I do."

"You can stop trying to convince me, Seth, I'm on board."

"Great! Now all we have to do is solve this murder."

"Seth, please don't make light of it. Wait — do you think Larry knows something, or saw something? Is that why he's uncomfortable about being so exposed?"

"I suppose it's possible, although I find it hard to picture. I mean, he's been around this area for a while, but it doesn't seem like he's made many connections. Christopher, of course, but friends? I mean, buddies to hang out with? Or a girlfriend?"

"Or boyfriend," Meg added. "Maybe he's just being discreet. Or maybe he's simply not interested in a relationship with anyone. I've tried to give him his space, and it's none of my business, as long as he does what the job requires."

Seth seemed to choose his next words

carefully. "Will that change when he's living twenty feet from the house? Do you think you have the right to know more about him under those circumstances?"

"Like what?" Meg challenged him. "That he's a serial killer? Or transgender? And isn't it illegal to ask questions like that of a tenant?"

Seth held up both hands. "Whoa! I wasn't exactly serious. Look, I like the kid. He seems like he needs a break. His personal life is his own business, as long as it doesn't endanger anyone or anything. But I'm not going to ask Art to run a criminal background check on him, or ask Larry if he likes to set fires for fun. Sometimes I like to rely on my own gut."

Meg smiled. "What women would call intuition. Do I think Larry Bennett is a threat to man or beast or property? No, I don't. And I'm happy to leave it at that."

"Then we're on the same page. Anything you need to do today?"

"I told you, I want to bake cookies. Lots of cookies. So when family, friends and law enforcement officials show up at our back door, I've got something to offer them."

"Sounds good to me."

8

As Meg had hoped, everyone in Seth's family was available for dinner on Sunday. She was including Christopher in the mix, although he wasn't quite officially family — yet. He was possibly the most likely person to have other commitments, since the spring semester at UMass had just begun, but his responsibilities were now more administrative than academic, so he could be flexible. And luckily, everyone in the family enjoyed his company.

Such an odd in-between time February was. In New England spring was nowhere in sight, but the days were beginning to get longer. No sign of buds on her apple trees yet, but she didn't want to hurry them along, because a sharp freeze at the wrong time could destroy the season's crop. So everyone was waiting, fidgeting, until things warmed up and the yearly cycle could begin again.

Meg had polished all the downstairs surfaces — amazing how much dust accumulated over the winter, thanks to a busy furnace. When days were short and often dark, it was easy to ignore, but once she pulled back the curtains and threw up the blinds, it was painfully obvious. She made a note to herself to wash the curtains too — she had inherited them and wasn't even sure they were washable, but they definitely attracted and held the dust. Why was it women were so concerned about keeping a house clean? She counted herself as one of a long line of farm women, who were responsible for keeping the families — and possibly the hired help — fed and clothed and healthy, and most likely raising chickens and tending to the garden that was a primary food source for the family. Oh, and birthing the babies, and taking care of the aged relatives. Why had they decided that dusting and scrubbing should be added to that list? Or was that what the "hired girl" was for? A young girl from the neighborhood, or maybe a distant relative that was one mouth too many for her family to feed, would learn the skills she'd need for her future role as farm wife by starting with the basics. At least Meg had a dishwasher and a washing machine and a vacuum cleaner.

She should count herself lucky.

And, she reminded herself, she was the one who had suggested this get-together. The gathering of the clan. Celebrating the vernal equinox, just a bit early. The blessing of the apple trees. Whatever.

The cleaning took no more than half the morning, so Meg put together a hearty stew and set it on the back of the stove to simmer slowly. She hoped Rachel's two older children would eat it — she made sure there were plenty of potatoes in it, if they didn't want to chew on meat. Then she rummaged in her refrigerator and discovered that she still had a few of the late-ripening apples from her own orchard: Northern Spy, notoriously finicky about producing at all, but when they did they went all out, which was why she still had some on hand. Apple cake, then, with plenty of caramel drizzle, one of her favorite recipes.

Seth had absented himself from her manic preparations. Not that he wasn't good at cleanup around the house, but he was really fired up about this tiny house idea, and now he and Larry were out back taking measurements and trying out bits of lumber to see what would work. She'd included Larry in the dinner invitation, mainly because it seemed rude not to. She'd always included her former orchard manager, Bree, in gatherings like this, but then, that was when Bree was sharing the house with Meg. Now Bree was off learning new techniques and ideas in Australia, of all places, thanks to a contact of Christopher's. Whether she'd be coming back — and in what role — was unclear, so Larry was filling her place, at least for now. Bree and Larry came from very different backgrounds and had their own ideas about how to run an orchard, but since Meg had started with zero experience in or knowledge of agriculture, she was grateful for any help she could get. And she thanked the heavens regularly that Christopher had come with the package, since her trees had once been the experimental and teaching orchard for the university's agriculture program. How quickly things had changed!

Lydia and Christopher were the first to arrive — not a surprise since they'd come on foot. "We're early, I know," Lydia apologized to Meg, "but we decided to walk over and wanted to get here while the light held. We'll cadge a ride home from Seth, if you don't mind. Do you need any help?"

"I think it's under control. I was complaining to Seth that without all the demands of the orchard I don't know what to do with myself, so I decided to cook. I may have made enough for an army. And I realized that we hadn't seen much of each other since the holidays. Are you keeping busy?"

Was Lydia blushing? "We've been cleaning out the attic recently. It's amazing how much stuff accumulates in a house over time. It seemed like so much space when Seth's father and I got married, and now it's crammed to the gills. But every time I start sorting something, I get sidetracked by memories, or I find something I had forgotten I had, so it's not going very quickly."

"There's no rush, is there? Heck, I've never really dug down to the bottom of the piles in the attic here. Who knows what treasures lurk? My mother was more the 'let's get rid of it now' school, although sometimes my father restrained her."

"What's going on out back?" Lydia asked. "Seth seems to have grabbed Christopher to explain it all to him, whatever it is."

"What, we haven't told you about Seth's latest project? He's at loose ends too, which is dangerous, so he decided that he wanted to create a tiny house, using the old foundation from the chicken coop. He figures Larry can live there, at least for now."

"Oh, right — I think he mentioned something about that. It won't be very big, will it?"

"No, but Larry's wants are simple. By the way, I invited him to come to dinner — it seemed unkind not to."

"How are things working out with him?"

"Pretty well, I think. He definitely knows his apples, but he's not terribly sociable. Not that that was a job requirement. He kind of seems younger than he is — I gather he spent much of his early life working on the family's farm."

"Well, as long as he gets the job done for you, it's fine, right?"

"It is. What about you? Are you working at all now, or are you a lady of leisure?"

"A bit of each. I still take on a few accounting jobs now and then, but only if I want to, and I keep my own hours and can work from home. I guess we're alike that way — if all I had to do was sit around the house and read books, I'd go mad fairly quickly."

The menfolk came bustling in then — Seth and Christopher had been joined by Larry, and even as they came in they were debating the pros and cons of various heating systems and construction materials. Larry was as animated as Meg had ever seen him, which was a good sign.

Seth greeted his mother with a hug. "Did Meg tell you about our project?"

"She did. Sounds like you're having fun."

"I think we are. It's kind of like a large toy, or a model. Did I make stuff like that as a kid?"

"I think so. You're welcome to rummage around the attic and see if any of it survived — as long as you promise not to make a mess, and to take away whatever of yours you find. You've got more space than I do now."

"I'll put it on my to-do list. Meg, you need any help with anything?"

"Cooking's under control. You can set the table, and maybe somebody could build a fire in the parlor?"

"Coming up!" Seth led his troops toward the front of the house, and Meg and Lydia smiled at each other.

"Since you're not driving, would you like a glass of wine or something?"

"That sounds lovely. If my nose doesn't deceive me, we're having something with beef and something with apples for dinner."

"Bang on. Red or white?"

"Red, please. I drink white in summer."

Meg had finished pouring two glasses when there was a commotion at the front of the house. From the sound of youthful voices, Meg deduced that Rachel and her family had arrived. From the sound of enthusiastic barking, she knew that Max had joined the fray.

Rachel's older children, Chloe and Matthew, came racing into the kitchen. "Can we go see the goats?" Matthew demanded breathlessly.

"Sure, as long as your uncle Seth goes with you. And he might have something else to show you out back." Meg glanced at Seth, who looked pleased by all the ruckus.

"Sure. How long until dinner?"

"No rush — stew can wait."

"Then we'll set the table when we come back in. Come on, guys — the goats are waiting."

"Put them in the barn before you come in!" Meg called out to Seth's retreating back. The door slammed behind them all.

Rachel peeked in. "Is the coast clear?" she said in a stage whisper.

"The kids are going to go harass the goats. Want me to hold Maggie while you take your coat off?"

"That'd help." Rachel disentangled baby Maggie from her carrier contraption, which seemed to involve a lot of straps, then handed her to Meg. Maggie studied Meg's face, then reached out and grabbed Meg's nose. Meg smiled at her and made a silly noise, which made Maggie smile back.

"She's grown so much!" Meg said.

"Yeah, they do that. You two given any thought to having one of your own?"

"Thought is about all we've given it — it's still an open question."

"Try it, you'll like it. But I promise I won't nag you about it. And you can borrow Mags any time you like."

Rachel draped her coat over the back of a chair and dropped into the chair. "So, anything new? How's the new guy working out?"

"So far, so good. He know his apples, but he's still kind of shy around people. I figured I'd stick him in the middle of dinner tonight and let him sink or swim. He knows Christopher already, and he'd better get used to the rest of you. You want something to drink?"

"Nonalcoholic, please. I'm still nursing Maggie."

"Well, I've always got cider," Meg told her, smiling.

"Fine."

It took the better part of an hour before everyone was gathered around the table in the dining room. Meg realized that hadn't bothered her a bit: everyone was happy, the food was cooked but not overcooked, and she reveled in being with family and friends. This, apparently, was one of the pluses of having free time. Not a lot, but enough to create a warm and welcoming atmosphere — and some hearty food. Maybe going back to simpler ways was a good thing.

The kids were excited by the plans for the little house that Seth had shown them. "It's so cool!" Matthew exclaimed. "It's like a real house but for small people. Like Chloe and me. Uncle Seth says that Larry's going to get to live in it! Can we have one, Dad?"

Noah laughed. "There you go, Seth — your first customer. But you'd better start saving your allowance now, Matt."

"Okay," Matthew said calmly. "You think we'll have enough saved up by summer, when school's out?"

"We'll see," Seth said. "I've still got to figure out how to make the first one."

While Maggie slept in a lined basket, the talk around the table ranged widely, from weather predictions to politics to the orchard business. By the time everyone's plate was cleaned, Meg realized that nobody had mentioned the murder in the backyard. Probably out of consideration for the kids, although Meg suspected that they would have heard something about it at school.

But probably not exactly where it had happened. She hadn't thought to ask Rachel or Noah whether it would be all right to talk about it in front of them, but she realized that she wanted to clear the air — and to talk with Christopher.

"We've got apple cake for dessert. Kids, would you like to take yours into the front room and watch a video or something? We grown-ups must be boring you by now."

"Okay," Chloe and Matthew said, nearly in unison.

"Take your plates out to the kitchen, then, and I'll cut the cake."

Rachel was eyeing Meg oddly. "What's up?"

"I wanted to talk about the shooting," Meg said in a low voice, "but I wasn't sure that the kids need to hear it. It won't take long, but you need to know that it took place only a few hundred yards from here, out back."

"Oh, God," Rachel said. "I'm so sorry to hear that. But you're right — the kids don't need to be part of this discussion, although no doubt they've heard some rumors."

"So let's dish up dessert and Seth and I can tell you what we know, and what's going on."

9

In the kitchen Meg doled out slices of cake, and added some ice cream to the children's pieces. They retreated happily to the front room, where they wouldn't be likely to overhear adult voices. Rachel checked on Maggie, who was, for the moment, sleeping peacefully. "I won't guarantee that she won't wake up in the middle of all this," Rachel told the group around the table. "You'd better talk fast."

"Don't worry. As I said, we won't take long," Meg replied.

Larry had been hovering on the fringes of the group, but now he said, "Do I have to stay for this? I don't know anything that you don't, and I've already heard it all."

"Go ahead, Larry," Seth said. "I only wanted to make sure that my family knew what was going on, rather than be surprised. See you tomorrow?"

"Yeah, sure." Larry ducked his head by

way of farewell, then grabbed his coat and headed out the back door.

When everyone was settled around the dining room table, with cake and coffee in front of them, Meg looked at Seth and said, "You should start this."

"I know," he said. Then he turned his attention to his family members. "Maybe I should start by asking, what have you heard, on the news or in the paper?"

Rachel snorted. "Sorry, but with three kids, one an infant, who the heck has time for the news?"

"Okay, fine," Seth said. "Please don't be hurt that I told Mom first, but she was bound to notice the police activity, and I didn't want her to worry. So, Meg and I were out walking around dusk on Friday and we heard a shot in the woods to the east. We didn't think a lot of it, since it is hunting season, although it sounded like it was pretty close to populated areas, which isn't legal. I was thinking about mentioning it to the Town Council, and then Max took off like a shot toward the woods, and I had to follow. Bottom line, I found a body in the woods. I'll skip the less-than-pleasant details, but it was a woman about my age who appeared to have been shot in the back. I never saw — or heard — anyone who might have shot her, and it had just begun to snow, so it was unlikely that there would be much in the way of physical evidence. Of course I called Art and waited for him to arrive, and he and his crew spent a lot of the night there. He called the state police, but they didn't get involved directly until the next morning. Meg and I came back here after Art arrived, and then Art and Detective Marcus dropped in the next morning and took my statement — Meg didn't have a lot to add, except for confirming the timing. After they left, we went over to Mom's to tell her."

There was a moment of thick silence around the table. Finally Noah asked, "Do they know who the person was? Do they have any idea who might have shot her?"

Seth shook his head. "The narcotics unit seems to be calling the shots. They know enough to say that it appears to be a murder, rather than a stupid hunting accident. I wondered how much the police have released to the public, other than that a shooting took place, with one fatality. Even saying the victim was a woman would make that statement more troubling. I'm sure they don't want people to panic, and most people around here are used to taking extra precautions during hunting season."

Rachel spoke up for the first time. "I cannot believe that you two are smack in the middle of another investigation of a suspicious death."

"Rachel, we're not exactly in the middle of it — nobody's asked us to help. It's just an odd coincidence that it happened on our property here," Meg said firmly. "I'm sure that the detective would be happy if we stayed out of it altogether."

"But . . ." Seth began, somewhat reluctantly. All heads swiveled toward him. "Much as I hate to admit it, there's something to be said for local participation. I'm not saying that our neighbors should be out poking around the underbrush looking for shell casings, but I did come up with one useful observation that might have escaped Marcus's notice."

"What was that?" Noah asked.

Seth looked around at the people at the table. "All of us here have a pretty good idea about the lay of the land for our adjoining properties, and what lies beyond. Marcus doesn't come from here — in fact, I have no idea where he lives, but it's not in Granford. I took a look at an aerial shot of our road here on the computer, and I realized that maybe the shot we heard might actually be no more than a random shot, *but* that the body could have been shot almost anywhere and carried in from the main road east of here and dumped where I found it. If you look at the images, it's all wooded on the north side of the road, and those woods form the boundary of Meg's property here, running toward the north. If the killer had picked his time right, no one would have noticed him going into the woods, with or without a body."

"Hold on," Noah interrupted. "You're saying you think somebody planned this? Committed the murder somewhere else and decided this would be a great place to dump a body? Aren't you making a lot of assumptions? Why do you think it *wasn't* a simple accident? Some idiot hunter took a shot he shouldn't have, in poor light, and when he found out what he'd done, he left in a hurry."

"I'm not saying that isn't the case. All I suggested was that, given the almost total lack of physical evidence, it makes sense to look for alternative explanations, rather than just jump on the simplest solution. We here have what you might call insider knowledge that the police don't. Art might, because he's been here a long time, but he doesn't know this end of town well. Look, nobody would be happier than me to find out that this was an accident, and the shooter has come forward and confessed and the case is closed. You know I don't go looking for trouble."

"You don't have to," Rachel said. "It finds you anyway, dear brother. So what is it we're supposed to do with what you've told us?"

"Nothing," Seth said firmly. "This hasn't made the news yet, which is kind of surprising, but that's the way the narcotics people want it. Rachel, I think you and your family are safe in Amherst — nobody goes hunting in the middle of town. I'm sure your kids' schools take hunting season into account when they plan field trips, and it's still too early in the year to be thinking about outdoor events. Mom here is more exposed. The deer-hunting season is over, although there are often a few hunters who'll take their chances off-season, but I'd guess that most hunters will steer clear of this neighborhood now, after what happened. There's not much game here in any case. All I really wanted to do was to alert you if all this happens to show up in the papers and you read that Seth Chapin of Granford found a body in his backyard."

"Believe me, Seth, we do appreciate that," Rachel said. "And I hope this will all be wrapped up quickly."

Baby Maggie had started making little mewling noises. "Somebody sounds hungry," Rachel said. "Maybe we should head for home."

"I'll round up the kids," Noah volunteered.

Seth stood up. "I'm sorry if I cast a shadow on what was a very nice dinner, but I thought you should know what was going on."

"That's okay, Seth — it was the right thing to do," Rachel told him. "Take care, all of you."

After a flurry of sorting out coats and hats and scarves and baby gear, Rachel and family departed into the darkness. Christopher and Lydia were starting to make similar leaving noises when Seth stopped them. "There's something else I wanted to talk to you about — particularly you, Christopher — that I didn't think Rachel and Noah needed to hear. Mind if we sit for a little longer?"

"Anybody want more coffee?" Meg asked.

"Sounds as though we might need it," Lydia said ruefully.

When everyone was settled again, Seth began, "I didn't exactly give the whole story, in part because Detective Marcus told me not to spread it around. He shared this only

108

because I was the one who found the body, and he knows he can trust me. I don't know if he's hoping that I'll remember something important, or that I know more than I'm telling him, or that he only wanted to be polite."

"Will you get on with it, Seth?" Lydia demanded. "Otherwise we'll be here all night."

"Fine. The state police do know the identity of the dead woman, and have almost from the beginning. She was an investigative reporter from the *Boston Globe*, working on a story about the steep rise in opioid trafficking in the Pioneer Valley. She was undercover, but she did clear it with the state police, specifically the narcotics unit, so Marcus had met her."

"Ah," Christopher said, "that does shed a different light on things."

"It does. One, it makes it much more likely that she was killed deliberately and dumped here, because her killer thought nothing in this area would point to anyone remotely known to the police. Two, this simple idea is made more complicated because whoever dumped her here had to have known at least something about this area, to know there would be enough cover to conceal what he was doing. I'm going to assume that no criminal goes wandering around in the half dark with a bleeding body in his car looking for a good place to hide it, where it might not be found for a while."

"So you're saying it could be a neighbor?" Lydia asked.

"Not necessarily a current neighbor, Mom," Seth said, "but someone who's been around here before." He glanced at Meg. "But I have to admit, this whole thing has been a real wake-up call. To tell the truth, I had no idea we had anything like a serious drug problem around here. Maybe I've been living with my head in the clouds, but I can't recall anyone mentioning it. Maybe that's what happens when you work for yourself and you don't have kids in the school system. But just because I'm blind to it doesn't mean it isn't happening. That's one reason I wanted to talk to you, Christopher."

"Me? Do you think I'm a drug dealer?" Meg had to look closely to see if Christopher was joking; it appeared he was.

"Of course not. But you are part of the university, which means you see a lot of younger people all the time. Have you noticed any change in behavior in them, over the past couple of years? Acting oddly? Furtive? Falling asleep in class? I wish I could be clearer, but I'm clueless about what substances are available and what the symptoms are."

"Seth, while I am no expert, the university does circulate warnings to the staff and faculty. I know enough to say that the entire drug trade is much more sophisticated than it used to be, and dare I say, more subtle. Much of it, or so I'm told, is focused on prescription drugs, obtained illegally. Tracing those is a very different problem than searching for the source of, say, heroin. So there is no one single avenue for illicit drugs, there are many, and they are diverse."

"I'm sorry I'm sounding like an idiot. I guess you raised me right, Mom — I never messed with drugs when I was younger — or now, for that matter. And I understand that the market has changed radically."

"I'm glad I did something right," Lydia told him, smiling.

Seth turned back to Christopher. "So I guess what I'm saying is, you have a broader access to relevant information than I do. Will you keep your eyes and ears open and let me know if you notice anything? Or if the university issues some urgent message? Because, unlikely though it seems, it could have something to do with the Granford killing."

"Of course I will, and I'll share with you whatever I learn. But it is quite apparent that we all should be observant these days, and not dismiss what we think we see as paranoid fantasy. I will admit it saddens me to say that. But it appears that evil has arrived on our doorstep."

"I'm afraid it has. Look, are you ready to go home? I'll be happy to drive you back."

"Thank you, Seth," Lydia said. "I'd appreciate that."

"Meg, you okay with that?"

"Sure, as long as you leave Max here to protect me. He can slobber an intruder into submission." *But,* she added to herself, *he won't be able to stop a rifle bullet.* "Go!"

Meg went outside to wave goodbye to Lydia and Christopher, bringing Max with her. She sat on the back steps, watching Max sniff his way around the yard before he did his business. It was still cold and very quiet, except for the occasional car passing and Max's huffing sounds. She could hear the goats munching hay in the barn. It looked so deceptively peaceful, and yet a woman had died a few hundred yards away.

Had somebody found out who she was and what she was doing in the area? Had she messed up and let something slip? She was old enough to be experienced — she wasn't an eager rookie reporter looking to make a big splash. How long had she been under cover? The longer she sat, the more questions she came up with, and at this rate she'd never sleep. She whistled to Max, who came loping over to join her, then went inside, making sure the door was locked behind her.

10

Meg had gone to bed early the night before, after cleaning up the kitchen with Seth's help. She hated to come down to a kitchen full of dirty pans and plates covered with congealed food, no matter what the time. Still, in spite of plenty of sleep, she felt kind of draggy in the morning.

It had been nice to spend time with Seth's family members. At least, the first half of the dinner had been nice. The second half had been less so, but it was better to get everything about the murder and the investigation out in the open now. Maybe somebody with fresher eyes would stumble over a clue that would crack the case, and they could all move on.

Downstairs Seth had already made coffee and was reading the weekly edition of the local paper. Getting the daily paper in print wasn't possible in Granford but Meg hadn't gotten used to browsing online — she still preferred paper, and she'd been a daily reader for most of her life. Was she still clinging to a bit of her Boston past? Certainly there wouldn't be much Granford news in the *Globe,* unless the murder and the identify of the victim had been revealed. Who knew the identity of the dead woman, so far? Marcus did, because Jenn had told him who she really was, in confidence. Somehow Meg doubted that he had spilled the secret to anyone else, since the narcotics unit had asked him to keep it quiet — that wasn't his style. At some point either the local police might figure out who she was, or someone from the *Globe* would come looking for her, if, say, she'd told her editor what her plan was. How secretive had she been? Meg reminded herself to try Googling her to see what information came up. Was Jenn in fact a seasoned reporter? Meg had only other people's comments to go by.

Meg filled her mug and sat down across from Seth. "Weather's not bad."

"Nope, sure isn't. Larry coming back?"

"Yup. You two are supposed to play with your tiny house. How long do you think it will take to put it together?"

"Not long. There are some good plans available — what Norm Abram would call a 'measured drawing' — so I don't have to reinvent the wheel. I've already bought some of the structural lumber."

"The kids seemed to like the idea yesterday."

"Funny how differently they reacted to it. Chloe liked the idea better than Matt."

"Hmmm." Meg took a sip of coffee. "Wonder how Bree's doing?"

"You want her back?"

"Not exactly. She's smart and hardworking, but she needs to add to her orchard skills. The fact that she's a woman of color may make getting a job more difficult. Or she may fall in love with Australia and decide to stay. But I did enjoy working with her."

"Not Larry?"

"I don't know him well yet. He's certainly got more experience. How long do you think it will take me to catch up?"

"Got me. Do you want to?"

"Catch up? You mean, rather than just hiring people to do the real work, and strolling around the orchard pretending to be queen of the hill? I feel responsible for the trees, and making this all work financially, but I know there are things I need to learn if I'm going to be directly involved. You going to keep renting out your house?"

"Do I need to decide right now? I'd hate

to sell it — it's been in the family forever. But it's not like we need it. It can bring in a little extra money if I rent it out, but that comes with management responsibilities that I'm not sure I want. It's been less than a month since I found some tenants, not that it would be hard in this area. I think I'd like to see how the semester goes before I decide."

"Works for me. Just don't send me over to clean up after the tenants. All guys?"

"So far. So it's either up to them to keep the place clean or they'll have to bring in someone from the outside to do it, and pay out of their own pockets."

"Do they all have cars? Do they carpool?"

"Meg, I didn't ask. There are buses to Amherst and the other colleges, you know."

"No, I did not know that. I've never needed one."

"Now you know. But otherwise, I'd like to assume that twenty-something young men can look after themselves. Maybe I'm naïve. I'll try to check in with them now and then, and if they're trashing the place, I'll boot them out. I think there's a clause in the lease that lets me do it."

A knocking at the back door startled them, and Meg was surprised to see Detective Marcus on the stoop. Seth went to let him in. "Detective. Can I hope you bring good news?"

"Sorry, no. Meg, I wanted to talk to you about your orchard manager."

"Larry? Why? Wait — you want some coffee? Can you sit down for a few minutes?"

"Fine."

He sat and watched as Meg busied herself filling another mug with coffee. She placed it in front of him, then resumed her seat. "What do you want to know? Oh, and is this an official part of your murder investigation?"

"Potentially. Your orchard manager, Larry Bennett, lives in the house up the hill. Did anyone there ever mention seeing Jenn? Did you never see her anywhere around here?"

Meg shook her head. "Larry had never mentioned it to me. And I haven't even seen a photo of the woman, so I can't say I saw her — or her body either. I'm beginning to get the feeling that a lot of people pass through that house. Detective Marcus, why haven't you revealed her identity to the news? It's bound to come out sooner or later."

Marcus didn't meet her eyes. "As I told you, the narcotics unit has requested that we withhold that information for now. That is all that I'm authorized to say at this time."

Interesting. Meg filed away that fact for later consideration.

After a pause, Marcus spoke again. "As part of this investigation, I've been looking into the people who were located closest to where the body was found. Obviously that includes you and Seth, and Seth's mother. And you've told me that Larry is currently living at your former home, Seth."

"Yes. I'm renting him a room. There are a few other tenants there as well, students at Amherst College or UMass, and one guy with a job."

"I was not aware of that until quite recently — I'll have to talk to them. Have they been living there long?"

"No, about a month, from the start of the semester. They paid rent for January."

"Can you provide their names?"

"More or less. I didn't do anything like a background check. I did interview them personally. But I'm new to this landlord business, so I can't swear that I asked the right questions."

"All males?"

"Yes, that's who applied. Larry was already living there by then."

"You can't see who's coming or going from down here, can you?"

"It's over the crest of the hill, so no, and

the front door faces the road up there. There's a partial view from the second floor here. Are you planning to ask my mother these questions? Her view is about as good — or bad — as mine."

"If it comes to that, I'll be discreet."

Meg could tell that Seth was getting impatient. "Why don't you cut to the chase, Detective? What do you want to know?"

"I would like to know if any of those young men, Larry Bennett included, knew or had contact with Jenn Chambers."

"So ask them. I mean, you didn't show a picture of Jenn around publicly, right? And it hasn't appeared in any news source. You said you were keeping a lid on that, at the request of the narcotics unit, to protect the investigation."

"And I have. So?"

"Has anyone from any department of the police gone around asking members of the public if they recognize her? Because if they don't, it's going to look kind of funny. Unusual, at least. And definitely suspicious."

"Chapin, we know our jobs. It's likely the woman had contacts in different parts of the community. She was trying to fit in. Maybe she looked for a job, or went to the library. Of course some people may have seen her."

"Did she use her real name? Or a fake one?"

Detective Marcus's face was growing redder by the minute. "I'm not obligated to tell you about our procedures. What's your point?"

"Seems to me like this is a pretty half-assed investigation, and people in the community may notice that. And it's the narcotics people who are running it. As far as I can tell, they know less about Granford than you do. You know, Larry's the least likely guy in the bunch to have had any contact, deliberate or accidental, with Jenn Chambers. Larry Bennett is not local. Sure, he's been in the area for a while, but it's not like he grew up here, and the time he's spent here was mainly in a lab at the UMass campus. He doesn't have a wide circle of friends, and he's not exactly a warm and friendly guy. The other three are much more sociable, if the partying that goes on is any indication."

Meg saw the flaw in Seth's reasoning just before Marcus opened his mouth. "Detective, do you have any reason to suspect Larry of dealing drugs? Any evidence? I'll admit that if that was the case, Larry and Jenn might have crossed paths. But I don't think it's likely."

If Marcus was fixated on Larry, there wasn't a lot she could do. Meg took a deep breath. "So you want to question Larry?"

"I do. I realize that both of you are on his side, but that has no legal bearing on the investigation. I'm not planning to arrest him, just talk, but I do need to find out if he had a connection with Jenn. And I'll ask the same questions of the other occupants of the house. Do you know where I can find Larry?"

Seth answered him. "If he's not up at the house, he said he'd drop by here this morning — we're working on a project together."

"And we're planning the spring orchard activities," Meg added. "Do you want us to tell him you need to talk to him?"

"I'd rather you didn't. I'll find him soon enough."

"Do you seriously think he's going to go on the run simply because a police officer wants to have a conversation with him?" Meg demanded.

"Meg, I admire your trusting nature, but I may know more about his background than you do, and I'm not predisposed to trust him." Marcus stood up abruptly. "I should be going. I'll let you know what develops."

Seth saw him to the door, then shut it

after him and leaned against the door to look at Meg. "Every time I think that guy might be half human, he goes back to cryptic mode. Why couldn't he have simply taken 'no, he's not here' as an answer? But no, he has to drop hints about something dark in Larry's past, and then he doesn't want either of us to clue Larry in."

"Are we going to?" Meg asked.

Seth looked at her levelly for a few moments. "He's your employee, so you have the right to choose. You have more to lose."

"Seth, that's not fair! We may not know Larry well, but Marcus doesn't know him at all. Christopher vouched for Larry, and I think Christopher is a good judge of character and a fair-minded man. If there's something in his past that is sketchy, I'd like to hear Larry's version before I throw him to Marcus."

Seth finally smiled. "Meg, don't bite my head off. I happen to agree with you. Of course, Larry may not want to share all his dark secrets and may run anyway, but I'd like to give him a chance."

Meg smiled back. "Good, because that's what I think too. Look, whenever he shows up, would it be better if you talked to him, man to man, or should I do it? I'm not even sure where or how to start."

"Well, you can try the obvious: ask him if he knew Jenn."

"Seth, that won't help much if he lies."

"Oh. Right. So what do we do? Wait — have we ever seen him with a girl?"

"He's almost thirty — I believe the correct term these days is *woman*. But I rarely see him except here. He did say something about not liking all the noise and stuff that the guys at the house make. He didn't mention any women there, though, although I assume there have been some. I really don't feel comfortable with this. I want Larry to believe that I trust him, if I'm going to be working with him."

Seth smiled. "I think we're caught in the middle. Marcus is the steady, stern grown-up, and Larry is secretive. They're not going to mesh well."

"That's all too true. So, we're going to talk to Larry, and then we'll decide whether we should share whatever information we get with Marcus. Or maybe Art."

"I hate to throw cold water on this, but how much do you trust Larry to tell you the truth?"

"Seth, I really don't know."

11

Their conversation was interrupted by the arrival of Larry knocking at the back door. Whatever else he might be, he was punctual and reliable. And Meg didn't seriously consider him a killer. Did she? Marcus had planted the thought in her head, but he'd been wrong before. But she would have to tread carefully with both Marcus and Larry. Here she'd thought that retiring to the country and tending trees would give her a simpler life, but that certainly wasn't working out.

She decided to pretend things were normal. "Hi, Larry — you eaten breakfast?"

"Yeah, I'm good. Seth, you up for getting started?"

"Sure," he said, with an enthusiasm that only Meg would recognize as slightly forced. "Did you have any new ideas after thinking about the layout?"

"I'd vote for keeping it simple. I like the

125

two-story idea — putting the bed in a loft up above. But downstairs I don't need much — kitchen, bath, and a room with someplace to sit, maybe a table."

"For one person, or more than one?" Seth asked.

"Like a round table, maybe. More than one chair, but some that could be put out of the way. Look, I don't have a lot of company."

Seth replied, "Still, if I want to show this to other people, so they know what's possible, they'd probably expect a table with two or four chairs. Don't panic — I wouldn't just barge in on you with snoopy people, and we're a long way from finishing it, much less giving tours. Call this an experiment. If there's something you don't like, it'll be easy enough to change. What kind of windows do you think you want?"

"Uh, well" — obviously Larry hadn't thought about that detail — "not too big, to save heat. But enough for some good light. At least there's nobody who could see in, in any direction."

"True. How about a porch in front?"

"Why?" Larry looked bewildered.

"It would make it look more finished, without a lot more work. Give another place to sit, when the weather's nice. Oh, and I'd

stick storage spaces inside wherever possible, built in. I know you don't have much
stuff, but other people might, in the future."

"Oh. Yeah, I can see that."

Poor Larry, Meg thought. He seemed so
out of his depth. Had he never considered
how he wanted to live? She wondered if he
even owned pots and pans to cook with, or
plates to eat from. There wouldn't be room
for a washer unless . . . "Maybe a stackable
washer/dryer. Mini-fridge or larger?" Meg
asked.

"I don't eat much," Larry said.

"I'd get a small one for now, but leave
room for something larger in the future,"
Seth told him. "Ready to go?"

"Yeah, sure," Larry said.

"While you two big strong men are out
there laying out the place and sawing wood,
I'll make lunch," Meg said. "Isn't that my
job?"

"Sure, after you've milked the cows and
baked six pies," Seth said, grinning. "We'll
be back in a while." Seth led Larry out the
back, talking about measurements and materials.

He's really into this project, Meg thought.
And why shouldn't he be? He liked to keep
busy, and he liked to make — or repair —
things. And this was a practical solution to

what would probably be an ongoing problem. With Bree Meg had been able to offer a room and all the conveniences of a house, but now that wouldn't work, so her employee, whoever it was, would have to fend for himself. The tiny house was a kind of compromise. Even if Larry left at some point in the future, it could still serve as a guesthouse, or worst case, as storage. And knowing Seth, even the outside would be carefully thought out and well assembled — nice to look at. She turned to study the contents of her refrigerator, thinking of what could go into a hearty soup. Lolly checked out what she was doing and went back to sleep, and Meg rubbed her head before returning to menu planning. Soup with corn bread on the side, she decided — she knew she had plenty of cornmeal.

Chopping vegetables gave her time to think. Or forced her to think — she'd already been doing too much of that lately. It had been a hectic few months recently. Getting married to Seth had certainly been a major distraction, but, she realized, she'd known him for quite a while by the time they had decided to make it official. It hadn't been an overnight decision, or a moment of headlong passion. In fact, he hadn't much liked her when they'd first met —

how trite was that? She wasn't looking for anything like a relationship then, and he'd already been divorced. But things had kind of happened, over time. She'd gotten to know his family, and he had encountered hers, in the midst of a murder investigation. She'd struggled to figure out how to run an orchard, and he'd given her space to learn — not that he knew any more about growing apples than she did. They'd built a foundation for a life together step by step, without hurrying.

So why had she made such a leap of faith with Larry? She'd gone solely with Christopher's recommendation and her gut. Well, for one thing she felt sorry for Larry. He was pretty close in age to her, but he seemed oddly naïve, and kind of lost. She hadn't wanted to pry about his upbringing, but she'd gotten the impression that it was lonely. He had trouble making friends, or maybe he simply didn't want to. She wasn't about to judge him as long as he could do the job she'd hired him for, and Christopher had promised her that he could.

But had she failed to do her homework? Job application? References (beyond Christopher's)? Academic record? Did he, heaven forbid, have a criminal record, juvenile or adult? Marcus would find out easily, if such a record existed. She'd kind of thrown herself on the mercy of fate, hoping for the best, and shutting her eyes to the worst. It had worked pretty well — until now. Still, while she respected Marcus's abilities as a police officer, she didn't quite trust him as a judge of character. He wasn't the type to fixate on the first available suspect, but neither was he equipped to understand the real person, and certainly not on short acquaintance. "Just the facts, ma'am" — wasn't that a catchphrase from some old television show? Facts had their place, but so did empathy. Seth definitely had more empathy than Marcus. Meg was glad he was on her side about Larry — and had her back. Now there was a muddled metaphor.

She went back to chopping. Onions, carrots, dried beans, herbs, stock. Potatoes could go in later. Maybe it wasn't an inspired mix, but it was hearty and filling. Good country food. Well, she was a farmer. She'd said so on her tax return!

A couple of hours later Seth and Larry came back in. Larry looked more animated than he had earlier. Maybe he and Seth had bonded over carpentry. "Something smells great!" Seth said.

"Soup and corn bread. I could make brownies for later, unless of course you've finished the whole thing already."

"Not quite. Larry's going to make a run to the box stores to get some items I forgot. He can look at appliances while he's there."

"Sounds like a plan," Meg said, ladling soup into earthenware bowls. "Eat first."

It didn't take long for the soup to disappear. Larry finished first and carried his dishes to the sink. "I'll head out now," he told Meg and Seth, "so maybe we'll have some time to work some more after I get back, while there's still light."

"Thanks, Larry," Seth said. "Why don't you take the truck? Here are the keys." He tossed a small bunch to Larry, who caught it skillfully in one hand.

"See you later," Larry said as he left.

Once Larry had maneuvered Seth's truck out of the driveway, Meg and Seth remained sitting across from each other at the table. "Anything to report?" Meg asked.

"Apart from the fact that I feel guilty trying to pry information out of Larry? I can't say he's hiding anything, or if he is, he's doing a good job of it. But he's pretty close-mouthed anyway, so it's hard to tell."

"What did you talk about? I mean, you did talk while you were measuring and cutting and all that stuff?"

"Some. You know, man stuff. We grunt

now and then, and point."

"You're kidding?" Meg asked.

"Of course I am. Mostly we talked about his life growing up, and how he learned about orchards. More the latter than the former. He didn't say much about his childhood, but I'd guess it wasn't exactly happy. To his credit, he didn't slander either of his parents. But it sounds like he didn't have a lot of friends, because he always had to help out on the farm. Maybe that's why he's having trouble adjusting to living in a house full of guys. He's just not used to it."

"Think he'll loosen up with time?"

"Maybe. I don't think he feels very secure about his life, where he's going. Like whether you'll keep him on. He seems to keep expecting the worst."

"I don't pick my employees based on personality, you know."

"Meg, you've hired all of two people — and both of them were more or less handed to you by Christopher. I'm not saying he was wrong about either of his candidates, but you can't exactly take the credit."

"Thanks for the vote of confidence. I could have said no." Could she? she wondered. "Bree worked out well enough."

"Yes, she did, but you were lucky."

"Seth, what are we talking about here? I

trust Christopher, and I want to think that most people are decent and hardworking and will do what they promise to do. Bree did. I want to believe that Larry will. So what's the argument here?"

Seth sat back in his chair and stretched. "Maybe I'm not being fair — to you or to Larry. But when somebody is found shot dead in my backyard, I start feeling suspicious of everyone. I don't like it. Plus — don't laugh — I feel it's my job to protect you."

Meg absorbed Seth's words with mixed feelings. First came happiness — it was sweet of him to worry about her. Second came annoyance: she was an independent woman capable of taking care of herself, and she didn't need a man to take care of her. Third came confusion: Was she supposed to thank him? Argue with him? Change the subject to something neutral like the weather? None of those seemed right. His response was predictable: caveman protecting his mate, and all those future generations of little cavepersons who would grow up to be modern Homo sapiens. And that's the way the human race was hardwired, no matter what feminists had to say. But wanting to protect her meant that Seth loved her, and that was worth something. Finally she said, "I hope I won't need that, but thank you. And I'd do the same for you, as far as I am able."

"If I remember correctly, you already have."

"Oh, right. Well, there was that. Don't let it be necessary again, please!"

He came around the table, and when she stood he wrapped his arms around her and simply held her, and she relaxed against him. *Yes, this is good. This is the way it should be. Just as long as he remembers I have a brain too.*

"So, what do we do about Larry?" he murmured into her hair.

Meg took a step back. "Way to break the mood, buddy! But if you're asking seriously, I'd say we tell him that Marcus is looking for him and why and see how he reacts. There might be a simple explanation. Or he might panic and walk out the door and disappear. If that happens, do we have to tell Marcus that we tipped him off?" *Tell him that we chose to bank on instinct rather than his rather sparse facts?*

"I hope not."

"Did you make a plan to get together with him again?" Meg asked.

"He's going to bring back the materials today, but I'm pretty sure it'll be too late to start on anything. The weather's supposed to be decent tomorrow, so we can start in the morning."

"Does he — I'm not sure how to put this — seem to feel a sense of ownership of the house yet?"

"Frankly I think he's incredulous that anyone would do something like this, just for him. Poor kid — maybe he's never owned anything, or never felt he belonged anywhere."

"He's not exactly a kid, but I know what you mean. Do you think he'll loosen up once we get to working in the orchard?"

"Maybe. I hope so. He's a good kid."

12

After a quiet evening, Meg and Seth went to bed early, and the next morning Seth was already up and bustling around in the kitchen below when Meg woke up. Meg was happy to see that the day promised to be sunny, which meant that Seth and Larry could make some progress on their construction project. She assumed Seth was handling all the permits and permissions to move forward, but given his position as councilman in the community, he'd do it all by the book. Which was as it should be. He was an honest guy, and he wanted people to know that.

She scrambled out of bed, threw on some warm fleece clothes, and went down to the kitchen. Max was asleep on the floor, next to his empty dish. He looked up when Meg walked into the kitchen, but once he'd identified her he went back to sleep, so Seth must already have fed him, or he'd be gnawing eagerly at her ankles. Lolly didn't seem to be hungry either: in her favorite nook on top of the refrigerator she was busy giving herself a thorough bath. Meg looked out the window and was not surprised to see the goats munching on their daily allotment of hay. Where did Seth find the energy to get all these things done? At least she could tell that he'd eaten breakfast — and hadn't washed his dishes. So he was human after all.

She could hear sounds of voices out back, but no sawing or pounding sounds yet. There was no need to rush, and she did believe in the old adage "measure twice and cut once." She helped herself to coffee, made some whole-wheat toast, and sat down at the table to figure out what she was supposed to be doing. She hoped there would be time for a walk-through of the orchard with Larry soon. She knew it was still early in the season, but they needed to prune the trees before they started budding. But she also knew that each year there were some trees that would have to be replaced. It hurt her to condemn a tree, but if they were too old or unhealthy to bear fruit any longer, they had to go. She was running a business, not a safe haven for old trees. Was there anyone around Granford who made furniture or household items like bowls? Would they like some seasoned applewood? Worst case, she could save the cut trees to use for firewood next winter.

She was startled to hear knocking at the front door. When she reached it and opened it, she found a twentyish young man standing there, looking uncertain. "Is this where Seth Chapin lives?" he asked.

"Yes. Do you need to speak to him?"

"No, thanks. I'm one of the guys who lives up the hill in his house, and I'm just delivering the rent checks."

"Oh, right. Listen, are you in a hurry? Or would you like to come in and have a cup of coffee? Seth's out back at the moment."

"Yeah, sure, I guess. I don't have a class until ten. If it's no trouble." He carefully wiped his feet on the mat before stepping into the house.

Meg led him toward the kitchen. "Are you a student?"

"Yeah, at UMass."

"Please, sit down. What's your major?" Meg asked, finding a clean mug and filling it.

"Uh, English literature, but the old stuff, like *Beowulf*."

Meg refilled her own mug and sat down opposite him. "I'm sorry — I didn't even ask your name. I guess I'm not quite awake yet."

"Mike Wilson. I know you're Mrs. Chapin — I see you outside now and then. Cool goats."

"Call me Meg, please. I didn't plan to have goats, but I had to rescue them, and then I sort of kept them. They're interesting. So, you're, what, second or third year?"

"Yeah, third. It's great that your husband is letting us rent the house. If you show up around here at the wrong time of year it's hard to find a place to rent. I was in a dorm my first year, and I don't want to try that again."

"How many of you are there?"

"Well, me, and Larry — he works for you, right? — and two others. We didn't know each other before we all moved in, and we pretty much go our own way."

"How's that working out?" Meg asked.

Mike shrugged. "Okay, I guess. We each buy our own food, but nobody seems to want to clean up the place. But we're working on it. I mean, somebody's got to do it."

Meg shuddered to imagine the condition the place would be in after a couple of months of clueless single guys living there. "Are you all in school?"

"No. There's me, and Tom. Ed's got a job,

and then there's Larry, who works here. Easy commute for him." Mike smiled, almost bashfully.

"Well, I'm glad it's working out for all of you. This is the first time Seth's rented the place, but he doesn't want to be a hands-on landlord. He'd rather you took care of things on your own."

"Yeah, he explained that. We're cool with that. What is it that Larry does here? He doesn't talk much, not about himself."

"He's my orchard manager. I inherited the house and orchard from my mother, and I'm trying to make it work as a business. But I started out knowing nothing at all about agriculture, so I hire people who have the experience to guide me."

"So those apples on the hill are yours?"

"They are. But this is a small business — just me and Larry, and we bring in pickers from outside for the harvest season. Seth and I added some new trees last year, but it'll be a while before they bear fruit. Are you from around here?"

"New York State. I've seen plenty of apples, but I never thought about growing them."

"It can be hard work, but I like it. It's rewarding to watch them grow, as long as there aren't insect attacks or blight or drought. So far we've only had one dry spell, and there's a well up the hill we use to water the trees if we need to. This is only my second year, and I'm still learning."

Mike seemed to be getting twitchy. Was he having trouble talking to an "old" person? Was that what she was now? Meg wondered. A middle-aged farmer? She sighed involuntarily. "Well, I'll let you go. It's been nice talking with you, Mike — it's good to know who your neighbors are. Just give me the rent checks and I'll make sure Seth gets them. And let one of us know if there are any problems up at the house."

Mike bounced to his feet, looking relieved, and handed her a slightly crumpled envelope. "Sure will. Thanks a lot. It was nice meeting you."

"Did you drive over? You can walk through the orchard to your place if you want to take a shortcut."

"Yeah, I drove. I'm heading for campus from here."

"I'll let you out the front then."

Once he was gone, Meg went back to the kitchen, feeling restless. Like Seth, she really wanted to be doing something useful. But she couldn't exactly help Seth and Larry build anything, and she needed Larry's input if she wanted to look at the orchard and figure out what to do next. Did she need any tools? Or was she supposed to sharpen the tools she had? Her mother certainly hadn't prepared her for farm life.

Her choice was taken from her when she looked out the back door to see Art arriving. She put the kettle on to boil for more coffee before she let him in.

"Good morning, Art! At least I hope it's good, or relatively good. No new bodies?"

"No, just the one. And before you ask, no, we haven't released the woman's name, but I can't say how long it will be a secret."

"Why do you say that? Oh, you want some coffee?"

"Always. I say that because there's a guy who showed up at the police station in town yesterday and asked where he could find Jenn. He described her pretty well, so he probably did know her. I'm wondering how he knew to come here to Granford to look for the woman."

"What did you tell him?"

"I waffled. He seemed to know that a body had been found, but I said we had not confirmed the dead woman's identity."

"And he accepted that?"

"He didn't argue."

"Has he talked to Marcus?" Meg poured him a cup of coffee — was this already the second pot of the day? — and warmed it up in the microwave before sliding it toward him.

"I can't say, and Marcus doesn't usually volunteer any information to me. I suggested the guy talk to him, in Northampton, but I don't know if he did. I bet Marcus is going to be pissed off if he does — he'll either have to lie or turn the guy over to the narcotics unit."

"Why do you say that?"

"Sounds like turf wars to me. Marcus handles homicide, but narcotics has grabbed the lead on this. The two units don't seem to play nicely with each other."

"They've got different agendas, I assume. Does this new guy seem to know anything?"

"He said his name was Justin Campbell and he kept his questions pretty vanilla. Like, 'Have you seen my girlfriend? She said she was coming to Granford for' — you can fill in whatever lame reason you like — 'but I haven't heard from her for days and I'm getting worried. She said she was visiting friends out this way, but she's not answering her phone.' "

"You're not buying his story?"

"Not really. People — especially the ones younger than I am — seem to communicate compulsively on their cell phones these days, like every few minutes. If his story is for real, there are probably multiple reasons why she wouldn't stay in touch with him, and not answering her phone might be her way of cutting him off. Maybe she dumped him. Maybe he's a stalker. I'm happy to help, but I don't hand out information all that freely."

"So he said she told him she'd be in this area," Meg mused, almost to herself. "Do you think he knows what she was doing here?"

"Hard to say. But the fact that he's here at all bothers me. Maybe he's legit, but she's dead and that's a pretty big red flag. Before you ask, he did *not* ask the obvious questions about the body of a woman that was found here. Like, did she match his description of his missing girlfriend."

"Is he the only person who's come looking for someone?"

"As far as I know, but hey, I'm one of those old fogies and I'm law enforcement. There are some people who would go out of their way to avoid talking to me. And if there's anything off about why she's here, they'd be even less likely to ask me to help find her. Unless somebody wants to make it known that she's dead."

"Art, I don't envy you — this seems to be

getting more and more complicated. But whatever his intentions, I'd guess this guy, whoever he is, doesn't know how small rural towns work. He's a stranger and he can't exactly hide it. Does that suggest that he's a city guy?"

"Maybe. I don't know. Does it matter? We know where she came from. But the general public doesn't. And while his questions hint that he knows something, I can't prove it."

"I don't know — I'm just tossing out ideas. Art, why are *you* here? Is there something you want me to do?"

"I guess I just need somebody to talk with, bounce ideas off of. Marcus won't talk to me, or the drug unit told him he can't, and I don't know what I'm supposed to say or *not* say because I don't know who knows what. I can't exactly ask this stranger — who's doing nothing wrong — what he's doing in my town. Sounds like a bad TV Western, doesn't it? You see any way to get him talking without scaring him off?"

"Run over his foot in your police car? Sorry, kidding. Have you done any searches on his name?"

"Not yet. Why do you want to know?"

"Because maybe you could find him online, if you know his name."

Art sighed. "I still have trouble thinking of

the internet first. I must be getting old."

"Hold on!" Meg stood up quickly. "I've got an idea. Follow me."

Meg went to her computer, still on the dining room table, and turned it on. Once it was warmed up, she searched on "*Boston Globe* Staff" and clicked on a link. Then she turned the screen to face Art. "These are pictures of the *Globe* staff. See anyone you recognize?"

Art fished a pair of reading glasses out of his shirt pocket, then peered at the screen. "There's Jenn, although her hair is different in the picture. And . . . damn, that's him!" Art pointed to one small picture among the page of journalists: Justin Campbell. "So there *is* a connection and he's here looking for Jenn, maybe because they were working on the same story? I mean, did this Jenn person tell him where she was going, but without any detail? She worked for him? He looks kind of young, so maybe he worked for her? Or maybe they had a personal relationship?" he suggested.

"I think Marcus should know about this."

"You're probably right. If this guy started looking in Granford maybe Jenn told him she'd be here, or near enough. Wonder if he knows she's dead? Or if he's made a leap of logic because he knows a body was found here?"

"If he knew she was here and he knows that a woman died here, he's probably put two and two together," Meg pointed out. "He is, after all, a journalist."

"So why didn't he go to the state police and ask? If he was in fact a friend of hers."

"Maybe he thought the state police would see through his story, assuming it was false. Sorry, Art, but he may think they're smarter than you are."

"And if he came here first he'd find a crotchety old police chief who didn't know much but wouldn't have any reason to disbelieve him — that would be me."

"Maybe he's trying to save the story?" Meg suggested. "I mean, if the state police know who she was and haven't made that public, he must figure they've got a reason not to release that information. Maybe he was working on it with her. Or maybe he wants it for himself. If he's figured out that the state police are sitting on this, he must assume it's juicy."

"Great," Art said glumly. "That might even give this guy a reason to kill her. So we've got a possible lead on the killer but no way to follow up on it. I should just hand him over to Marcus?"

"That would be the responsible thing to do. You are, after all, an officer of the law."

"So I'm told. I wonder if they're going to want me to go find him, and then tell him that the state police want to talk to him, and maybe they'll ask if he knows who might have killed her?"

Seth came barging in the kitchen door and stopped when he saw Art. "Something going on?"

"Nah," Art said. "I just wanted to pick your wife's brains — they're better than yours anyway. Larry with you?"

"I came in for some more coffee. He wanted to keep working. Want to see what we've done?"

"Maybe later. Let me fill you in about what Meg and I have been talking about."

After Art had wrapped up his summary, Seth said flatly, "If he's honestly concerned about her, he'd talk to Marcus, or someone else in homicide. If he comes up with a different story, you and Marcus can compare notes, maybe suggest some other angles."

"This guy might still be protecting the story, if he believes there is one. So he could be lying too."

"Right — visions of Pulitzers dance in his head. Or he might kill you to shut you and your overactive imagination up."

148

"This is why I love working with you guys — you're so optimistic." Art stood up stiffly. "Thanks for the coffee, Meg. I guess I'll see if I can track down Marcus and tell him what little I know. And hope he doesn't laugh at me."

"Good luck, Art."

13

"Well, that was odd," Seth said, draining his coffee.

"Kind of. When did life around here get so complicated? Used to be if a stranger wanted some information about who lived where or where to find the library, they'd ask someone on the street, or maybe the police station. Then GPS happened, so nobody talks to anybody. Now Art's got himself tied into a pretzel trying to figure out what to say or not say. And Marcus may not pay any attention to him anyway if he tells him about this Justin guy."

"I know," Seth agreed. "Those two got off on the wrong foot somehow, or maybe it's just Marcus, because Art's one of the nicest guys I know, and he's not stupid. But what's worse, it sounds like Marcus is butting heads within his own police department."

"You mean with the drug unit? I wonder who decides whether to ignore an inconvenient murder in order to pursue a bigger investigation into local drugs, because that's what it sounds like. The two are quite possibly connected, and Marcus knows that. Do you think the state police are up to the job of sorting all this out?"

"Let's hope so."

"Oh, one of your tenants stopped by to drop off the rent checks. Mike, he said his name was."

"At least he's on time. I know their names on paper, but I'm not sure I can put faces and names together. I make a lousy landlord, don't I?"

"It might be one chore too many for you. Although I understand why you don't want to leave the house empty, especially in winter, and why you're not ready to sell it. What's your mother think?"

"She leaves it up to me — my name's on the deed."

"Well, this Mike said he's a student at UMass, and so's one of the other guys. Then there's Larry and the fourth guy, who have jobs. From what Mike said, it sounds like they're all struggling with working out how to keep the place clean. I wonder whether if they pooled their resources they could afford someone to come in and clean, maybe every other week?"

151

Seth seemed interested. "You have any idea what that might cost?"

"No," Meg told him, "but I can find out. Split four ways, it can't be too bad, can it?"

"Got me. But since I'm the landlord, I can insist that they pay for it — or just raise the rent to cover it. Should I ask Larry to dinner tonight? I'd like to hash over what we've done today, so we can get an early start in the morning. Weather permitting."

"No problem, except that I have no idea what we're eating."

"You'll figure it out." Seth drained his mug and headed out the door again.

Once again Meg found herself alone, wondering how to entertain herself. She'd already vetoed doing anything that involved paint or solvents inside, because she couldn't open the windows for ventilation. It was too cold to paint outside, although at the very least the trim could use it. She could sort through the miscellaneous junk in the attic — Seth had added a number of boxes since they'd been married — but the temperature would probably be below freezing up there. There was nothing that needed doing in the basement. She could go up to the orchard and give her dormant trees a pep talk. She could learn to knit. Or she could clean house.

Wasn't free time supposed to be more fun than this?

Maybe she should go to the market and find some food. She could find a recipe for an elaborate dessert that would need half the day to assemble and cook. That would take until dark, at least. It was a plan: go find raw materials, then make food. But first she wanted to get some exercise, and taking a walk up the hill to check out the orchard seemed like a fitting idea.

She added a few layers of clothes and some sturdy boots, found her bag (when was the last time she had needed it?) and hat and scarf and gloves, and set off up the hill. She was panting only slightly by the time she reached the band of trees that ran along the west side of the orchard. She turned to survey her small empire, tucking her hands under her armpits to keep them warm. Close to the field to the north was the former chicken coop, rapidly morphing into a human living space as Larry and Seth bustled around it. The basic framing was coming together quickly, and she watched for a while as Seth and Larry performed some sort of elaborate dance, handing each other tools and pieces of wood, then stepping back to admire the results. They looked happy.

Meg turned in the opposite direction. There was Seth's house, now more or less a dormitory, or maybe a boardinghouse. There was only one car parked next to it, which Meg recognized as Larry's; the others must be at work or classes. Beyond that, farther north, was Lydia's house. Those two houses were the only neighbors she could see in that direction, although Meg knew it wasn't far to a more settled road that led toward Granford. Looking back down the hill, Meg studied the band of trees where Jenn had been found dead. In the bright sunlight the cover looked sparse — anyone walking through there, especially someone carrying a body, would have been very obvious if anyone had chosen to look in that direction. She tried to remember if she'd ever looked at it by dusk or night and came up blank. A flashlight would be obvious, of course, but she had trouble picturing anyone moving a body while holding a flashlight.

She still came back to the idea that someone had to know the immediate geography to choose to dump a body there. It couldn't have been accidental. But was it spur of the moment? Even she could come up with a number of other local sites that would have been better suited — there were plenty of patches of woods and brush around Granford, and there was even a convenient river a bit farther away. Had the killer been forced to hurry? Why? Had Jenn found something damning that demanded that she be silenced quickly, with only sketchy planning? Had she sent anything to Justin, if they were in fact collaborating somehow? Or to her editor? Who else might know what she'd found?

Had she kept a computer or a tablet with her, to record her findings, or had she judged that to be too dangerous, if somebody found it? Or maybe someone had found it and taken it away or destroyed it. Had this woman ever gone undercover before, or had she been so eager that she had ignored her own safety just to get the story? The make-or-break story that would bring her fame and glory and maybe a permanent niche at the paper — if anything at newspapers was permanent anymore. Now it was all live streaming and podcasts and such. The thought brought her to a stop. She'd had the brainstorm to look for the mystery guy asking questions in town by going to the paper's website — but she hadn't looked up Jenn online. It was unlikely she'd posted important details, but there might be something in social media or even on Google that would give a clue about how

Jenn operated, what interested her, and how she communicated. Meg couldn't access anything with a password, but she could certainly look at public records, past history and such.

With a last glance at the landscape spread out below her, Meg turned and loped down the hill. Time to go online. *Not such an old-fashioned farmer now, are you, Meg.*

Two hours later it was getting dark outside, and Meg had a half-inch stack of printouts next to her computer. And she couldn't stomach looking at one more article on the screen. How much information was too much? She'd gathered a lot of basic facts: Jenn had been about Meg's age, as she had guessed. She wasn't married, and she lived in Boston. References in the paper's archives showed she'd been writing feature articles for them for about five years, and had been a contributor to earlier articles. Justin appeared to have contributed to a couple of those.

The earlier articles had most likely been assigned, and they were a hodgepodge of restaurant reviews, coverage of suburban events like parades and significant funerals, and the occasional short piece about topics of general public interest. Nothing unexpected popped up. Over the years Jenn had drifted toward harder-edged stories and the occasional editorial. She'd put together a nice solid career for herself. Why had she decided to commit to a bigger subject? Had she hit some sort of ceiling, or was there a personal reason? Maybe Justin would know, if anyone ever tracked him down.

Had Art in fact talked to Marcus about Justin? Would Marcus take their information seriously? He'd made it clear, time after time, that he resented the interference of outside amateurs, no matter how often they had contributed significant clues. Now he had his internal turf wars to fight, and this time it was made more complicated by departmental infighting. But if they did turn up something important, like Justin's presence in Granford, Marcus shouldn't be blindsided by something he needed to know, coming from one of them. They had to get along with him for the foreseeable future.

The sun was pretty much gone when Meg looked at her watch. Crap, it was past five, and she'd promised dinner to two men who'd been working outside in the cold all day. They'd be hungry. What could she throw together quickly that would fill them up? Spaghetti, she decided. With some kind of sauce, based on whatever was handy. And a bottle or two of red wine — although she couldn't remember seeing Larry drink anything alcoholic, he did seem to favor the idea of a cider operation using her apples. But not hard cider, she assumed — that came with all sorts of regulations.

The phone rang as she was filling her largest pot with water to boil the pasta. "Hey, Art, what's up?"

"Not enough," he said glumly. "I told our favorite detective about the guy who'd been asking about Jenn, and that we'd identified him. He more or less patted me on the head and hung up. So much for our good deed of the day."

"You did the right thing, Art. And at least you tried — he can't fault you for that. We can talk more tomorrow — I've got some new ideas."

"Great. Just what I need. Tomorrow, then, Meg."

Meg hung up, then put the pot on the stove to bring the water to a boil. What did she have to work with?

It was nearly full dark when Seth and Larry returned. "Max was helping us out there," Seth said, "so he's had his exercise for now. I think he might appreciate his dinner about now, though."

"Great," Meg said. "You're way ahead of me. I got sucked into an internet search and lost track of time, but I'm making spaghetti with lots of sauce, and I found a loaf of Italian bread in the freezer, and I'm hoping I hid a cake in there somewhere so we can have dessert. Larry, you staying?"

"If you want me to."

"Fine with me. Seth said you still have some planning to do. How's it coming?"

"Pretty good," Larry said. "If we get decent weather we could have it livable by next week. At least, that's what Seth says."

"He's usually right," Meg told him. "Larry's a good student, and he works hard. You like what you see, Larry? Because if you want to change anything, now's the time to tell me."

Half an hour later they were settled around the kitchen table. Meg dished out mounds of cooked spaghetti and passed the sauce and cheese, while Seth filled wineglasses. "You want any, Larry?"

Larry shook his head. "I don't drink. My dad did enough for the whole family."

Meg's ears pricked up: that was one of the first personal remarks she'd heard Larry make. "I'm sorry to hear that. Did you have any brothers or sisters?"

Larry avoided looking at Meg directly,

159

choosing to poke at his spaghetti. "Nope. It was just me."

"So you and your father managed your farm, just the two of you?" Seth asked.

"Yeah." Larry did not elaborate. "Until he got rid of the place and moved into town. Didn't last much longer after that."

"I don't mean to pry, Larry. I just wondered where you learned about apples. You clearly know what you're doing."

"If I was out in the orchard I couldn't hear my folks fighting."

There seemed to be little to say to that, so Meg shifted the subject. "So it must be quite a change for you, to live with a bunch of other guys."

"Kind of. We're still working things out. They're okay, I guess."

"But you'd rather have a place of your own, right?" Seth said. "That's why you're helping with the tiny house."

"Well, yeah. I guess I'm kind of private. I don't mind being alone."

"Well, whenever we get the house finished, we can talk about finding a replacement for you in my house," Seth told him.

Larry looked at Seth obliquely. "You might want to check out the next guy a bit more."

"Why?"

"Some of the guys don't get along real well. I mean, take me — I'm quiet, and I don't exactly have a lot of buddies dropping by. But the other guys, there are guys and girls dropping in all the time, round the clock. And they can be loud."

"I hear what you're saying, Larry," Seth said. "I don't have a whole lot of experience finding tenants, matching up compatible people. And maybe I should set some ground rules — like no wild parties, if you like your music loud wear headphones, pick up after yourself. And be considerate to your housemates. Does that about cover it?"

"I guess," Larry said.

If there was something more Larry wanted to add, Meg thought, he wasn't ready to put it into words. This was a new situation for all of them, and they could wait to see how things worked out.

"Dessert, anybody? I managed to find some brownies buried in the freezer."

"Sounds good to me," Seth said.

14

Meg was washing the dishes, Seth drying, when Meg said, "That conversation tonight was kind of disturbing."

"I think I know what you mean, but in case I'm being stupid, you mind telling me why?"

"I feel sorry for Larry. He doesn't talk much about himself or his past, but from the crumbs he's dropped I don't think he had a particularly happy life before he left home. And he still has trouble connecting with other people. Don't be offended, but I wonder if sharing the house with three other guys is the best thing for him."

"I know," Seth said. "Maybe I didn't think the whole idea through well enough. But theoretically, isn't it better for him to be around other people and learn to get along than to maintain his isolation?"

"In theory, I guess so. But it depends on the individual. I'm not suggesting you do anything about it, but I'm pretty sure he'll be glad when the tiny house is finished and he can move into it. I think he'd move into it if it was no more than a tent at this point. Nobody's fault — I'm just observing, without a lot of information. But here's a suggestion: next time you look for tenants, say next fall, why not try all girls?"

"I'll think about it. I think there's one last glass in the wine bottle — want to split it?"

"Sure." When Seth had emptied the bottle into their glasses, Meg said, "I'm not sure what we do about the murder situation — it keeps getting more muddled. I guess that's what happens when the big mean outside world intrudes in our sleepy little village."

"You mean the drug problem."

"Yes. I don't think either of us is naïve, but it kind of crept up on us. Or me, at least. Our problem is, Marcus is in a difficult position, and the drug unit people don't know us and have no reason to trust us. I'm not saying I distrust them, but we're working on a different scale. For us it's more personal, and in more ways than one."

"Maybe it's the wine, but I'm not sure what you're saying."

"I don't really know. We know where Jenn came from and why she was here, because she told the state police, but it's hard to figure out where she fit here in Granford, and she might not have given the police the details of her plans. Did she know people here? How did she connect with the people she was looking for? Was she staying somewhere here, or just dropping by when she needed something? She must have thought she was safe because no one knew her, but clearly she was wrong, because *somebody* tracked her down here. Unless you choose to think that this was a completely random event. But as we keep saying, the murderer must have some local ties. And that kind of scares me. I don't like being scared in my own home. And I don't want to turn this place into a fortress, and I don't see Max as an attack dog."

"Killer goats, maybe?" Seth said, smiling. "They're probably smarter than Max."

"Maybe you're trying to make me feel better, but I still don't like it."

"You have any suggestions about what to do next?"

"No, I don't. Art's already sharing what he knows with us. I guess we try to keep the lines of communication open with Marcus and hope the professionals can sort things out. That's not our job, right?"

"Agreed," Seth said. "We about done down here?"

"If you'll take Max for one more walk, I'll put the goats to bed. Then I'll top off everybody's food bowls, and then we'll be done. Pretty close to farmers' hours."

"Deal." Seth collected Max's leash from where it hung next to the back door — he always made a point of bringing it on walks, since Max sometimes couldn't distinguish between friend and foe. The distinctive jingle of it brought Max to his feet, and he bounded out the door ahead of Seth.

Meg followed more slowly. February was such a dreary month, not quite winter but not really spring either. She had to wonder how many farmers went stir-crazy, cooped up in their homes waiting for the farming year to begin again. Maybe there were murder statistics about February deaths. Or maybe there was a jump in the birth rate in November each year.

The goats didn't seem very interested in her approach — Seth must have fed them well earlier. Meg leaned on the fence and contemplated them. She knew she didn't want cows, but the goats had sort of happened. They were pretty low-maintenance, and relatively smart, but she had no plans for them. She looked past them, beyond the fencing on the far side, and saw a brief flash of red in the dusk. The fox she had seen earlier? Was it taking up residence on her land, or just scouting good locations? If she was raising chickens she might worry, but she didn't think the goats would mind, and Max was far larger than any fox. Lolly was an indoor cat, so she wasn't at risk.

The fox emerged from the underbrush and stood still a moment, sniffing the air. Meg could have sworn it looked at her, but maybe that was just fanciful. When it disappeared back into the woods, Meg told the goats, "Okay, ladies, time to go inside." They seemed to nod intelligently, and then she guided them into their pen in the barn. "Sleep well." Goat Dorcas gave her a skeptical look before settling into her straw bed.

The next morning Seth and Larry were already out pounding on the tiny house framing when someone came to the front door and knocked. It had been a busy week so far, Meg reflected: people just seemed to keep showing up. Should she be worrying about letting strangers in? She hadn't since she'd arrived, but then, she hadn't had a murder on her property before. Luckily Max had roused himself to follow her to the door. A criminal wouldn't know that he was a very friendly creature and totally useless as a guard dog.

The caller this time proved to be a thirty-ish young man, neatly dressed in the standard uniform of jeans, ankle-high boots, and a couple of layers of shirts under an insulated jacket. Clean-shaven, neatly cut hair. He certainly didn't look dangerous, but who did?

But she recognized him from his photo on the newspaper website: Justin Campbell. What did he want from her?

"Can I help you?" Meg asked.

"I hope so. My name is Justin Campbell. I'm from Boston, and I've been trying to track down my girlfriend, Jenn Chambers. She told me she was coming to this area, but she didn't say where or for how long, and I haven't heard from her in a couple of weeks. I'm worried about her. Do you know her, or have you seen her?"

So this was in fact the mysterious boyfriend Art had mentioned — Justin had just confirmed it. Could she, should she trust him? There were questions she was itching to ask him, but she didn't want to mess up the ongoing investigation by giving away too much. But there stood Justin, shivering just a bit, looking appropriately anxious and concerned. She could manage the discussion, couldn't she?

"You want to come in? You look like

167

you're freezing."

"That'd be great. I didn't realize how cold it could be in this part of the state — in Boston I spend more time inside than outside."

"I'm not sure if I can tell you anything, but I'm happy to help if I can." *And I'm pretty sure talking to you will help me,* Meg added to herself. "Come on in. The kitchen's the warmest place to sit."

"Thank you. I appreciate it."

Meg led him to the kitchen and tried to put her thoughts in order while she made yet more coffee. Maybe she should just get a programmable coffee maker, with a large capacity — it would certainly save her time.

"This is a great house!" Justin said. "How old is it?"

"It was built around 1760, I think. That's before the town was incorporated. Not a lot has been changed since then."

"You live here alone?"

A distant alarm bell rang in her head. Why did he want to know? "With my husband. He's out back, working. He specializes in restoring old buildings, and he works out of his office in the barn back there." There, she'd fended off the nosy question. She hoped that Justin didn't leap to the conclusion that she'd just created an imaginary husband.

"Must be nice. Lots of old houses around here."

"Yes, there are. The one next door and a couple up the hill were all built by the same family, quite a while ago. So, what's going on with your girlfriend? Jenn, did you say? And why are you looking here?" Meg brought two mugs of hot coffee to the table and sat down across from Justin.

He avoided her look. "I feel really stupid, you know? I mean, Jenn and I have been together a year or two now, but we had this huge fight a couple of weeks ago and she walked out of our place. She said there was something she had to do out this way, but she didn't give any details. I can't say that I blame her — I know I can be kind of a jerk. But I didn't expect her to stay out of touch this long."

"Have you talked to the police? In Boston or out this way?"

"Well, I didn't want to make a fuss. I mean, she's a grown woman and a pretty independent one, and she would be really pissed at me if I sicced the police on her just because we had a fight."

"I can understand that." *No, actually, I can't: if I went missing for a week under those circumstances I'd want someone to be look-*

ing for me. "Has she done anything like this before?"

Justin shook his head vehemently. "No, nothing like this. And she's always got her mobile in a pocket, but when I try to call it goes straight to voice mail."

"Why did you come looking for her here in Granford?"

"Well, I don't know this area well, but I figured it'd be hard to find one person in Northampton or Amherst because they're both pretty big and there are a lot of people coming and going there — you know, students, tourists and stuff. I had the feeling Jenn just wanted to get away from me for a while and spend time in someplace peaceful. I'll admit we needed a break."

This Justin was being awfully self-effacing about all this, and Meg didn't trust him. "But she didn't know anyone in Granford? No family or friends? Because this isn't exactly a tourist destination, and there aren't many places to stay around here. Why would she come here?"

"I'm beginning to figure out that asking around here doesn't make much sense. Stupid of me, I know, but I felt like I had to do something. For all I know she's still in Boston, hiding out from me. Or she went to see her mother in Ohio — I didn't want to call her mother's house and upset her."

"You think she might have thought she'd like to stay around here for a while? Maybe get a job? What does she do?"

"This and that. Some waitressing. She worked in a department store over Christmas. Stuff like that."

Alarm bells were clanging in Meg's head, accompanied by flashing red lights. She hoped her expression hadn't changed. "How about you, Justin?" she asked. "Can you take much time off from work to look for her?"

"I've got an office job, working with computers, and I've got plenty of vacation time coming. It's not a problem. I just want to make sure she's all right. I'm not a creepy stalker or anything like that."

So you say. Meg took a long sip of her coffee while she sorted out her thoughts. She'd almost believed the sincere boyfriend shtick, but then he'd blown his cover by lying. Of course, he didn't know that she knew a lot more about what was going on than an ordinary housewife would have. "I wish I could help you, but as you've probably learned, this is a small town, and we don't get a lot of strangers here, so somebody would probably remember seeing her. You might have better luck looking in Holyoke. And you really should talk to the police here if you think she was headed to Granford. It's been long enough that they should take you seriously, and all you risk is embarrassment if she suddenly turns up."

"You're probably right. I'm sorry to have bothered you."

"Don't worry about it. Let me show you out." When he stood up, Meg led him back to the front door and held it open for him. "Good luck to you. I hope she turns up, safe and sound."

"So do I. Thank you for talking with me." He smiled politely, then turned and went back to his car. Meg watched as he got into his car, but after starting his engine he didn't drive off immediately. Instead he pulled out his cell phone and called someone. Was someone else waiting for his call? Meg watched until he pulled out of the end of her driveway, with a fake smile plastered on her face, before shutting the door behind her and double locking it. She thought for a moment, then pulled out her mobile phone and called Seth: she didn't want Larry to hear what she had to say. Not yet, anyway.

Seth answered quickly. "What's up?"

"I just had a very odd conversation with Justin Campbell — yes, that one, the so-called boyfriend. Don't say anything out

172

loud, because I don't want to involve Larry just yet, but I'd kind of like to talk with you about it, while it's fresh."

"Larry's gathering more lumber from the barn, he can't hear me. The guy was actually here? At the house?"

"Yes, he was. He seems like a nice enough guy, but he lied to me, to my face. Of course, he doesn't know how much I know, and I played innocent and sent him on his way. But I'd really like to talk to you, now."

"Be there in two minutes."

15

Seth had clearly been worried by Meg's cryptic comment: he was back in less than his estimated two minutes. "You okay?"

"Of course I'm okay," Meg said more tartly than she intended. "This Justin person seemed perfectly respectable and polite, and told a convincing story. Of course, he'd know how to do that if he's a journalist. But I knew he was lying. Not so much about who he is, but when he started talking about Jenn, he claimed she was his girlfriend and she worked at odd jobs like waitressing, and they'd had a big fight after which she walked out, and I knew most of that wasn't true. He didn't have a good explanation for why she would head to Granford, where it's kind of hard to hide. But of course, if she was chasing after drug dealers and he knew it, he'd want to stay as far away from any real explanation as possible. Wouldn't he?"

"Yes, I think so. So, in time-honored

fashion he just played dumb. 'We had a fight and she left and I haven't a clue why.' That usually works. Of course, it's often true: a lot of guys are clueless about why relationships go bad. So, tell me what he said."

"All of it?" Meg asked. "Or just the stuff he made up?"

"All of it. Please."

Meg ran through the details of Justin's visit, until she reached his first lie. "I swear I would have believed him if he hadn't lied to me then. He was definitely trying to fool me. What do you think he wanted?"

Seth sat back in his chair and thought for a long moment. "I would guess that he didn't expect to get any real information from you. Based on what Art said, he's already asked other people in town the same questions and gotten no results. Which may mean he knows that Jenn is dead and that her body was found awfully close to here and he's checking the place out. You didn't bring up anything about the murder, did you?"

"No way! I just pretended to be stupid. I don't know whether to be pleased or offended that he believed my act. Of course, he was acting too."

"Did he pay attention to anything in particular about the house?"

"Not the house, as such, but he did try to find out if I was living here alone, which I thought was kind of odd, so I said you were working out back. Anyway, he came in through the front, and he may have looked toward the woods, but that's something most people would do anyway. I wasn't watching him closely when he came into the kitchen, but he could have been checking out the views from the windows on that side of the house and what it would be possible to see, while I made coffee — my back was to him then. That's the problem I'm having: everything he did seemed perfectly ordinary, more or less what an innocent person would do. He didn't even comment on the goats or ask for a tour of the place. He asked his phony questions, thanked me politely, and went on his way. What now?"

Seth sighed. "I vote for calling Art. It'd be a waste of time to talk to Marcus just now, because he probably wouldn't believe you. Your story's pretty thin, and he could argue that you simply misjudged this Justin character."

"Yes, I could see that happening. You want to call Art or should I?"

"I'll do it." Seth got up, phone in hand, and walked into the dining room to call.

Meg didn't move — she just sat and

thought. She wouldn't have believed herself either. She wasn't exactly a skittish woman, fearful of strangers, jumping at every unfamiliar noise — and in a house this old there were plenty of those. But Marcus might not yet know her well enough to realize that. It would be much easier for him to dismiss what she said as the paranoid statements of a ditzy woman. Even one who had helped solve more than one murder with him.

Did this Justin look like a killer? No, he looked like a preppie. Of course, there were plenty of preppie killers, and their outward appearance and demeanor made it easy for them to get close to their victims. Meg hadn't paid much attention to Justin's listed credentials on the paper's website, but she'd be willing to bet that he'd attended an Ivy League school or two as he battled his way up the journalism ladder.

Seth returned quickly. "He'll be here in half an hour — he's got some other stuff to do. It's not like he's got any reason to arrest Justin."

"I didn't think he did. I do think Art needs to hear my story, that's all. It corroborates what he's heard from other people. I hate to throw cold water on all of this, but we're a long way from showing who killed Jenn. So this Justin knew her, and he worked at the paper with her, in some capacity. There seem to be a lot of people working there. We've been over this before — there are multiple reasons why Justin would be wondering where she was now, and not all those reasons point toward murder. I can't believe we're actually talking about this. It could be pure coincidence."

"Meg, do you really believe that?"

She didn't answer right away. Finally she said, "No, I don't. Too many coincidences."

Art's half hour dragged out to a full hour, and Meg threw together some quick sandwiches — and made more coffee. Surely there was something else she could be drinking, at least some of the time? But if she was honest with herself, she'd have to admit she was pretty much addicted to caffeine. She wasn't proud of it.

When Art arrived he came in the back, as usual. "So, Meg, you've got something for me?"

"Yes, I think so. I hope so. Before I start, do you have anything new?"

"I have learned a whole lot about drug trafficking and who's running the show for the baddies in Massachusetts," Art told her. "I don't recognize any of the players, and I haven't seen or heard of any of them in

Granford. For which I count myself lucky — I wouldn't want to mess with those people."

"Are they all scruffy thugs, or do some of them look like you and me?" Meg asked.

"Ah, Meg, don't take away my fantasies — I don't want them to look ordinary. I want them to look like criminals that I can spot from a mile away. I know, that's not realistic. So hit me with your story."

"First, can I get you some coffee?" Meg started out smiling, but after a couple of seconds she burst out laughing. "That seems to be the answer to everything. Any way to get truth serum into the stuff? It would make your job a lot easier."

"That it would," Art agreed. "But also kind of illegal."

"You're no fun! Anyway, here's what happened." And for a second time Meg outlined her encounter with Justin. Seth sat a few feet away but didn't interrupt. Art listened intently. When Meg finished, Art said, "He didn't do anything wrong, correct?"

"No," Meg replied. "He was polite, and thanked me. But he lied. He didn't know I knew he was lying. Why would he lie, if he didn't have some ulterior motive?"

"I can't say. I haven't had any other reports of a guy looking for his girlfriend

179

since the first one, and he certainly hasn't come to me. Neither of you mentioned the murder, right?"

"Of course not. Is there anything I should do?"

"Beyond telling an officer of the law who's a fringe member of the murder investigation?" Art smiled ruefully. "No, not really. I could pass it on to Marcus, but he's not particularly fond of Granford at the moment. The longer this drags on, the worse it looks for him. And me, for that matter, but nobody in town here expects me to solve a lot of murders."

"So I've done my civic duty, and that's it?" Meg asked, exasperated.

"Yup. I'm sorry, Meg. Your information may in fact be important, but Marcus is not in any mood to hear it."

"End of story," Meg said glumly. "Any drug busts locally?"

Art shook his head. "It's not like they've been bringing bales of weed or bricks of heroin worth millions into the area. Prescription drugs are more popular these days, I think, and much easier to conceal and distribute."

"Has anyone in Granford talked to you about drugs?"

"You mean, reported suspicious activity,

things like that?" Art asked.

"I suppose. I mean, I wouldn't know what to look for. All the cop shows I've seen seem to take place in a big city, in a neighborhood I wouldn't go near. It's hard for me to visualize drug dealers in Granford."

"Obviously looks are deceiving, if the narcotics unit is anywhere near right." Art sighed. "Anything else you'd like to say?"

"Not really," Meg told him.

Larry came in the back door and stopped when he saw Art sitting at the table. "Sorry, didn't mean to interrupt."

"That's okay — I'm about done here," Art told him. "Keep in touch, all of you, and let me know if you see anything or anyone suspicious."

"Thanks, Art. I'll walk you out," Seth volunteered.

"Do you want anything to eat, Larry?" Meg asked.

"Nah, Seth got some sandwiches. Who was that guy who stopped by earlier?"

Larry had noticed her visitor? Interesting. "He said his name was Justin and he was looking for his girlfriend Jenn. Art said before that someone had told him the same story, about a guy looking for a girl. This was right around the time Seth found Jenn dead. Why do you want to know? Do you know him?"

"No, but I've seen him at the house a time or two, in the past week, maybe. When I was around, I mean, which I'm not all the time."

Meg felt a small jolt of electricity. Jenn had died less than a week earlier, but Larry had seen Justin earlier than that? And in this neighborhood? Something didn't add up. "Does he know any of the other guys?"

"I'm not sure who he was there to see — mostly I stay in my room, when I'm not working here. Maybe he was just asking the same questions he asked you — where's his girlfriend. But he came by more than once. He's not from around here?"

"No, he says he's from Boston."

"Not a lot of people stop in Granford," Larry pointed out.

"True. They pass right through and go to Amherst or Northampton. Though now and then they stop at the restaurant here, thank goodness. I want that to stay open."

"I've never eaten there — costs too much."

Meg decided to change the subject while she digested what Larry had told her about Justin at the house. No point in digging for more information from Larry because he obviously didn't seem to have any.

"How's the tiny house coming?" Meg asked.

"Good. I've never watched anybody build a house from the ground up. This one's almost like a toy, because it's so little. But that makes it easy to understand how it all fits together."

"I'd guess it's a good place to start learning. With an old house like this, fixing or adding anything is always complicated because so many people have made so-called improvements in the past. And a lot of them were amateurs."

"I bet." Larry hesitated a moment. "You think it means something that this Justin guy was up at the house?"

So Larry had picked up on her reaction to that news? Meg considered how to answer. "You're saying you saw him more than once? And not just in the last week or so, but earlier?"

"Yeah, I think so. I wasn't writing down dates or anything. Hey, a lot of people come and go at the place. The guys like to party, and they've got a lot of friends. I don't know if they get any work done, at least the ones in school."

Something felt wrong about what Larry had just said. "When you say they come and go, do they hang around long, or are they in

183

and out?"

Larry shrugged. "I can't say — like I told you, I usually go to my room and shut the door when it gets crazy. And sometimes put on headphones. So I don't hear much."

Larry wouldn't hear cars coming and going. Meg was willing to guess that the guys who dropped by weren't there to see Larry, but she wasn't going to ask him. Why rub his nose in the fact that he didn't have any friends? "I know you have a car, Larry. Do the other guys?"

"Two of 'em do, but they're not always working. Mike doesn't, but he can usually get a ride from someone. Worst case, he walks up to the main road and catches a bus. Why do you want to know?"

"Just wondering. I don't notice much traffic down here, but mostly the windows are closed, and the furnace makes a lot of noise when it's running, which is most of the time these days. Maybe I'll notice more in the spring, when the windows are open."

"Why does Seth bother to rent it out at all?" Larry asked. "I mean, it's great for me, but it's got to be a lot of hassle for him. And you, I guess. Do you need the money?"

"Well, it's always nice to have a little extra money coming in, but I think Seth — who's a born and bred Yankee — thought it was a waste to see it sitting empty when he could make some cash from it. He'll probably sell it eventually, but he and his family have a lot of history there, and it's hard for him to give it up. And while his mother, who lives on the other side, says the choice is up to him, she might not want strangers as neighbors. You never know who you're going to get. It's all up in the air, anyway. We've only been married a couple of months, so we haven't made up our minds about what we're going to do."

"Sure — makes sense. Hey, I'd better get to work out back if we want to get this finished anytime soon."

"Go right ahead."

16

Meg and Seth ate a quiet dinner in the kitchen, trying to avoid talking about the murder. It wasn't easy.

"It seems like all we do is talk to other people, and each one contributes a very small piece of information, but I can't make all the pieces fit together," Meg complained. "And then there's trying to keep straight who knows what, and who *shouldn't* know what but does, and we can't talk about various things but we already know about them. The whole blasted mess makes my head hurt."

"I know what you mean. But what can we do about it?" Seth asked.

"Take a vacation in Alaska? Or find someplace where there isn't even a remote chance that somebody will want to give us another revelation that we won't know what to do with. Who was it that said that living in the country meant a simpler life?"

"Maybe it was a century ago. Not so much now. 'The world is too much with us.' That's Wordsworth, by the way."

"He died a long time ago. A lot of people died early back then. Are things better now?"

"Medically, I think so. As for the rest, who knows?"

Meg went still for a moment. "Was that a gunshot?"

"I didn't hear anything," Seth said, "but it could be. It's still hunting season for some things."

"How did I manage to live here this long and not know anything about it?"

"I assume that you didn't hunt when you were younger."

"I did not, nor did my father. Or mother, for that matter — I shouldn't be sexist. I'd bet women are more accurate shots than a lot of men."

"I won't argue with you."

"How about you?"

"I was never interested in shooting living creatures. Although I can see the argument for thinning out animals if they've over-populated an area. For example, you might have to worry about deer eating your apples, or even the bark from the trees, under the right conditions. Would that convince you to eliminate some of them?"

"Oh, great — something else to worry about. Maybe, since I assume the deer don't benefit from overcrowding any more than I would. Do people hunt deer around here? For pleasure, I mean?"

"It's permitted, but under very strict regulations, and only for a short time each year, with specific kinds of weapons."

"So overpopulation in this immediate area is not an issue?"

"Not for us, not here. Certainly not everywhere."

"So if what I heard was a gunshot, was somebody hunting legally? Illegally?"

"It depends. You'd have to do a bit of research if you really wanted to go out and kill something. Legally, that is. I won't say that everyone who hunts is following the laws."

"I'll pass, thank you. Well, maybe where rats are concerned . . ." Meg said dubiously.

"You haven't seen any, have you?"

"Not here, thank goodness. Seth, do you think I'm cut out to be a farmer?"

"You're serious?" Seth asked, startled by her abrupt change of subject. When Meg nodded, Seth went on, "You're not afraid of hard work — physical work, I mean. You're good with numbers, so you can handle the financial side of the business, which is something that farmers have to do these days. You know enough to ask for help when you need it, and you listen to advice. I guess it comes down to whether you like farming, or specifically, growing apples."

"I do, at least for now, in part because I like learning new things. Whether I'll feel the same way after five or ten years of it I can't say. But I don't have a plan for any other career."

"I'm sure you could find some sort of job at one of the colleges around here. You have the skills — finance, fund-raising, that kind of thing."

"I suppose. But that sounds kind of boring right now."

"And spraying for bugs and watering acres of trees isn't?"

"Not yet. You ready to go upstairs?"

"Without doing the dishes?" Seth asked, cocking an eyebrow.

"They won't go anywhere. I've got better ideas."

"Mrs. Chapin, you have a wicked mind."

The next morning Meg was downstairs before Seth and decided to take Max out for his first walk of the day. It was overcast, but she didn't remember any forecast for snow. She had mixed feelings about snow these days: too much made it difficult to get around or even get chores done, but too little meant having to water the orchard at critical times, which meant more work. Gone were the days when she could look out at a snowy landscape and simply think "pretty!"

Max went bounding around the backyard, but she knew he wouldn't stray far — he hadn't had his breakfast yet. Meg decided to go let the goats out, and make sure they had enough feed. It was an expensive indulgence to keep them and feed them, but she found them entertaining, and she didn't have the heart to get rid of them. Not yet, at least. Even though they ignored her as she opened the barn door and let them trot out into their fenced field. Affectionate they were not.

She shut the barn door behind them and checked the levels of feed — they could wait a little longer. Outside again, she walked along the fence line and leaned on the top rail to watch them for a few minutes, and to enjoy the crisp early morning air. Then she turned to go back to the house, but stopped in her tracks: her car was parked in the driveway, but one of the passenger side windows was a spider web of cracks, with

190

an inch-wide hole in the center. She uttered a curse that should have made the goats blush.

And then she remembered the gunshot that she might or might not have heard the night before. Could that have caused the damage?

Meg took a quick look around. As near as she could tell, the shot most likely had come from the same clump of woods where Jenn's body was found. But what had the shooter been aiming at?

She headed for the back door, fuming. Seth was still sitting at the table, making a list. He looked up when she came in and was quick to read her expression. "What's wrong?"

"There's what looks to me like a bullet hole in my car window, on the side toward the woods. At least, that's my guess. Either that or an elf with a very small hammer." She threw herself into her chair. "It had to be that gunshot I heard last night."

"Only one, right?" Seth asked. "I mean, it's not like somebody stood next to your car and let loose."

Meg shook her head. "Just the one, I think. What do we do now?"

"Call Art. It's either an idiot hunter, who should be tracked down, or it's malicious vandalism. He needs to know." He stood up to retrieve his phone but then stopped by Meg's chair. "Are you all right?"

"I'm not hurt, if that's what you're asking. And I didn't touch anything. I'm just mad as hell. And what kind of idiot is out there in the dark shooting at anything? Unless the guy was trying to send a message to me, or us. Which seems absurd."

"Come here," Seth said, and pulling her out of her chair, wrapped his arms around her. Meg realized she was fighting back tears, which made her even angrier. She hadn't asked for any of this. And she didn't even want to think what might come next.

She pulled away reluctantly. "Go. Call Art."

"I will."

Seth disappeared into the dining room, where he'd left his phone, and Meg decided to do the dishes from the night before — although she wasn't sure she could do it without smashing a few of them. What was happening? She'd been going along, minding her own business (in both senses of the word), and suddenly there was a body and weapons and drugs and too damn many questions to make sense out of any of it. Somehow she had inadvertently peeled off the pretty skin of Granford and revealed an unexpected darkness beneath. She scrubbed at caked-on food with more energy than necessary.

Seth came back. "He's on his way."

"What did you tell him?"

"That a shot took out your car's side window, but it probably happened last night. And it had to have come from near where Jenn was found."

"And that's all we know," Meg finished bitterly, sending water in all directions.

She was wiping up the mess she had made splashing water around when she saw Art's car pull into the driveway. He didn't come directly in, but spent a minute or two studying the damaged window, then surveying the area in all directions. The goats watched him with lukewarm curiosity. Finally he turned and headed toward the door. Seth let him in, and Meg wondered if Seth thought she would bite off Art's head if he didn't intervene.

"Morning, Meg. Notice I left out the 'good.' "

"Hi, Art. I don't have any right to be mad at you — you've been doing your job all along. I wish I could say the same of everyone else involved in this stupid investigation."

"Let's not get into personalities. Just tell

me the facts."

"Sit down," Meg said. She decided she was not going to offer him coffee again, not until this whole mess was cleared up. When Art was settled, Meg began, "We were eating dinner here at the table last night when I told Seth I thought I heard a gunshot. He didn't hear it. It sounded distant, not close to the house. And it had to have come from this side, because it would have been impossible to hear from the other side. There was only the one shot, and I didn't think anything more about it. This morning I went out to walk Max and let the goats out, and that's when I saw the window."

"What time was that shot last night?" Art asked.

"Probably between seven thirty and eight. I wasn't really paying attention to the time."

"Full dark?" he asked. Meg nodded.

"No curtains on the kitchen windows?"

"No, there's nobody who can see in. Most of the time, anyway."

"Sound like a rifle to you?"

"Art, I don't know weapons and I don't know what they sound like. It didn't sound like a handgun to me — they just go 'pop.' I assumed it was a hunter." Like she had when Jenn died, or was dumped. "Seth and I were talking about hunting regulations last night, but we didn't get into details."

"I assume he told you that there are a lot of requirements if you're planning to go out and shoot at things — legally, that is. First of all, you need a state hunting license. Depending on your target, there may be restrictions on what kind of weapon you can use, and when — during what hours. It may surprise you that the deer-hunting season is very short, and requires a special permit. It usually lasts only a week, or maybe a couple of weeks, in the fall. In any case, we're well past that now. Again, I mean legally. You're also required to keep a specified distance from settled areas — a hunter can't shoot a deer in your backyard. And there's no hunting for anything on Sundays."

"Who's in charge of enforcing all these regulations?" Meg demanded.

"Me. It hasn't been a problem. Until now."

Meg was beginning to cool down. "So are there any animals with a hunting season that's open now?"

"That you'll find around here? Foxes, mainly. We're in the middle of that season. You can get the licenses or permits online. And you can use a rifle at night. Between one-half hour after sunset until midnight you can use a twenty-two long rifle to hunt foxes."

"I have seen a fox around here a couple of times lately — I don't know if that was two foxes or the same one twice. Why would anyone want to kill them? Do they do much damage?"

"If you're raising chickens or quail or something like that, yes. Baby animals too, but it's kind of early in the year for that. Or maybe some fool just felt like shooting and killing something, and this was pretty much legal."

"Does that mean he'd have a hunting license?" Seth asked.

Art shrugged. "Maybe. I can check the database, but don't hold your breath."

"Art, let me ask you this: what kind of weapon killed Jenn Chambers?" Meg asked grimly.

Art hesitated before answering. "It was a twenty-two, fired from close range, and she didn't die immediately. She was shot somewhere else and dumped here to die, or after she was dead. And you didn't hear this from me, but I think you have a right to know."

"Based on the crime show reruns I've seen, that's a pretty small caliber, isn't it?" Meg asked.

"Yes. Can be dangerous up close. Or if it

hits a critical place and the victim doesn't get medical help quickly enough."

"What're you going to do now?" Meg said.

"I'll take a look at your car, get some pictures, so there'll be an official record. I can go over to that clump of trees and see if anybody left anything behind. But we may never know who fired the shot, and the jerk may be too embarrassed to come forward and confess. Or maybe he doesn't know he hit the car."

"Can I watch you?"

"Sure. You've got a good eye."

"Then let's do it," Meg said firmly.

17

The three of them pulled on their jackets and went out into the cold. Art pulled a small notebook out of a pocket. "Now, let me ask some basic questions, and then you can comment. Meg, do you usually leave your car in the driveway?"

"Yes, unless there's a blizzard coming. There's really not room in any of the other outbuildings to keep it there, and then I'd have to dig it out."

"So anyone driving by regularly would know it would be there," Art said, mostly to himself. "The bullet traveled some distance — if it had been closer, the window might have shattered into pieces. The bullet had lost some speed by the time it got this far."

"So the woods would have been a likely place for it to have come from?" Seth asked.

"Seems about right," Art said. "But I'm no expert. If there had been a fatality, the forensic people would be all over this. When you heard the shot, Meg, were you sitting at the kitchen table?"

"Yes. Oh, I think I see what you're getting at. Nobody standing in the woods over there would have been able to see us, or maybe just the tops of our heads. Are you thinking he wasn't shooting at us?"

"Go with the simplest explanation first, Meg," Art said. "Let us assume for now that he was shooting at one or more foxes."

"But the house sits a bit above the level of the woods," Meg protested. "There's a bog between — it's low there. Last time I checked, a fox was kind of low to the ground, unless they can climb trees. So to hit the car window, the person would have to have been pointing his weapon upward to some degree. Not near the ground where this hypothetical fox would have been. Unless the fox was sitting on my car."

Art smiled at her last comment. "Meg, that's a marvel of smart and ridiculous scrambled together. But I think you're right. Missing a fox — or even a deer, for that matter — would not have resulted in a spent bullet hitting your car window. The angle is wrong, although we have to take into account the possibility that the shooter slipped or tripped, and his weapon went off accidentally in the wrong direction."

"Are you going to look for the bullet?" Meg demanded.

"You have been watching your cop shows, Meg. I was just getting to that. Now, the bullet hit the near front window with enough force to penetrate it, but not enough to pass out the other side. Therefore it should be inside your car somewhere. Before you ask, no, you can't help me look — that would be contaminating evidence, if we decide to call it that. But I don't think I need to call in an entire crew to look for one bullet in a small car."

"Go for it," Meg said. "We'll watch."

Art was already wearing gloves. Meg didn't usually lock her car doors in her own driveway, so Art opened the front door where the damage was. It didn't take him long to find a small bullet lodged in the padding above the driver's side window. "Got it," he called out. "Seth, you got any skinny poles? If not, string would do."

"You want to check the angle of entry?" Seth asked. "I'll go get something."

He went into the barn, where his office was, and returned a minute or two later with several lengths of what looked like half-inch doweling. "Will this work?" Seth asked.

"Perfect. Now, if you wouldn't mind opening the driver's side window enough to get your hand through, I'll push this rod through from this end, and we'll see what direction the shot might have come from. Meg, you want to take pictures?"

"Sure, fine."

"Once you get enough shots of the interior and the exterior of the car, turn slowly toward the woods where we think the bullet came from. Make sure you turn without lowering the camera until you can see the woods over there."

"I get it: keep it level. Art, is this even legal? As part of an investigation, I mean."

"What, you think I need to call in CSI? I hate to tell you, but this is barely a crime. Our budget doesn't include high-tech investigations."

"Whatever," Meg muttered.

Art pulled out a small camera from a pocket in his jacket and handed it to Meg. She walked to the rear of the car, to a spot from which she could see the full width of the car, from entry point to where the bullet had ended up. She then swiveled to see how much of the woods she could see from that spot. Luckily there were no trees in the way. "Ready," she called out.

Art inserted the dowel and fed it through until Seth could grab the end and line it up with the bullet hole. To Meg's unskilled eye, it looked like the angle was about twenty degrees above level. She took multiple pictures, then she turned slowly toward the patch of woods, keeping the camera as level as possible, and snapped a few more pictures. As far as she could tell, there was nothing that ruled out a man standing among the trees and shooting a rifle directly at her car. Not at a fox.

"I think I've got enough," Art said. "I'm going to head down to the trees and see if there's anything like evidence there. You two coming?"

"Wouldn't miss it," Seth said. "Meg?"

"Of course. I've got to keep you two honest."

In single file they skirted the still-frozen bog. Meg noted that the peepers should be starting up soon, when the weather warmed up. They made a surprising amount of racket for a short period, but Meg found their sound charming.

Once they reached the tree line, Art stopped them. He looked up toward the house, with Meg's car parked on the side. "I'd guess the guy was about twenty feet in from here, based on the angle the bullet went in. Let's stick to this edge of the bog, in case there are any footprints or some such."

Once again Art walked ahead of them, his eyes on the ground, looking up at the house at intervals, until he was satisfied at the angle. "Okay, this looks about right. I'd assume he wasn't standing right here at the edge, even in the dark."

"Unless he was *trying* to hit the car," Meg grumbled.

"I told you, look for the most likely solution first. He thought he was shooting at a fox, we're guessing. Could've been a dog, I suppose — I'll check when I get back to the office to see if anyone around here has reported one missing, but it could have just run for home. But if the guy was shooting in this direction, he would have been back among the trees, maybe twenty or thirty feet. Someplace with a clear line of sight. Stay behind me."

They followed Art carefully through the trees until he stopped, his eyes roaming over the ground at his feet. "He could've taken the casings with him. Meg, you sure you heard only the one shot?"

"I'd say ninety percent sure. Once I heard it, I listened for another but it never happened. And as I told you, Seth didn't hear anything."

"Kind of odd, that he'd fire only once. If it was a fox he was firing at. I mean, even if that fox took off at a dead run, you'd think this guy would get off another couple of shots. If he was determined to get the critter, enough to come out at night, I'd expect him to follow through. Unless he was really scared of getting caught. Doesn't make sense." Art straightened up, stretching his back. "So, not much here to confirm our guy was standing here, but at least we have the bullet. If there's ever anything to compare it to."

"Is it rare?" Meg asked.

"Nope. It's pretty common. A twenty-two-caliber cartridge fits a lot of weapons. Doesn't cost much, and it's relatively quiet. Used a lot for small-game hunting. Not the best thing for long-range shots — it tends to drop down after about a hundred and fifty feet, so it's hard to be accurate from a distance. Which is about how far away your driveway is. So, please don't ask me to test every twenty-two rifle in Granford. I'd bet we'd find triple digits of the things."

Meg was feeling depressed. "So, what have we learned? Anything?"

"Given the distance and trajectory, I'd be inclined to say this was not accidental. Somebody fired at your car, but didn't intend to do a lot of damage. More like he was sending a message."

"What message? I don't see the point."

"Don't bite my head off, Meg. It could be that he isn't terribly familiar with hunting weapons, and he was only trying to convince you — and by proxy, me — that hunting does take place right around here, which lends some credibility to the idea that Jenn was shot by accident. He doesn't know that we know it wasn't. Maybe he thought we were village idiots and would simply assume it was an accident and close the case on Jenn. He might not have counted on us calling in the big guns — sorry, bad pun — to look at the evidence, which didn't show what he wanted."

"So, you're guessing that this was a guy who knows something about guns but wasn't used to hunting?" Seth asked.

"It's possible. Look, you two, I'm sorry I can't prove much of anything for you. I'm sorry your car is damaged. I'm sorry somebody dumped a body on your land. I'm sorry Marcus is such a prick and won't listen to any information that doesn't fit what he's looking for. You want more?"

Meg finally smiled. "No, I think that will do. Look, if we've seen all there is to see here, you want to go in and get something to warm you up?"

"Please!" Art said. "I can't feel my fingers

anymore."

As they trudged up the slope toward the house, Art commented, "You know, there are very few hunting fatalities in this country. Like, less than a hundred total, and some of those are due to hunters who manage to shoot themselves. I wonder if our shooter knew that piece of trivia when he dumped Jenn?"

"Art, I'm happy to concede that this killer isn't the brightest bulb, but so far he's gotten away with it," Seth said.

"I'm not finished yet," Art told him.

Once back inside the house, Meg asked, "At the risk of sounding trite, you want coffee? Or I could make something exotic."

"Coffee works for me," Art said, "as long as it's hot."

"I can guarantee that much. Won't take long."

Once they were settled around the table, with steaming mugs, Meg asked, "So Marcus is still stonewalling?"

"If that means taking orders from the drug unit and *only* the drug unit, and seething, and not sharing any crumbs he may have collected with me, then yes. His feelings are hurt. His ego is bruised. Pick your own terms — he's not a happy camper. For all practical purposes we're on our own here."

"Wait — there is something I meant to tell you, but I got distracted. You know that Justin Campbell came by the house here, claiming to be looking for his missing girlfriend. I played dumb and sent him on his way. You'd told me earlier that a guy — presumably Justin — was looking for a missing girlfriend."

"Yeah, so? Old news. What's new?"

"Well, I was talking to Larry yesterday, after you'd gone, and he asked who was the guy who had dropped by here. I told him and then I asked him why he wanted to know, and Larry told me that Justin had been hanging out at the house up the hill — Larry recognized him. But this was *before* we found Jenn's body, and more than once. You might want to talk to the guys up the hill again and see if you can figure out who knows Justin."

Art stared at the ceiling. "Let me get this straight. The story we've put together so far is that Jenn came to town looking for a big story on drug dealing in the area. She paid a call on the state police to alert them she was hanging around, and probably see if she could get any information from them, but as far as she knew, nobody in Boston, except maybe her boss, knew she was here. And then she turns up dead. Now you're telling me that this Justin knew, and he was already here before she died, and once she was dead he's been going around pretending he was her boyfriend and was looking for her. Were they working together, at least before she died? Was he trying to steal her story? Was he actually her boyfriend? A colleague? A collaborator? A competitor? What am I supposed to think?"

"Art, I don't know," Meg protested. "You know when Jenn first appeared here and talked to the narcotics unit. Larry might be able to put a date to when Justin first showed up at the house. The only way we'll know whether they were working together on this story or whether one was undercutting the other is to ask either Justin or the Boston editor."

"Or maybe the killer." Art stood up quickly. "Thanks for the coffee, Meg, and for the information. I'll go to the station and file an official report about the shooting — let me know if you need a copy for insurance purposes. And keep in touch — you seem to be coming up with more clues than I am."

"Of course, Art. Thanks for letting us tag along."

Once Art had pulled out of the driveway, Seth said, "Well, that was interesting."

"What, forensic analysis of crime scenes?"

"That and other things. Interdepartmental conflict, for example. Or criminals who think they're smart but don't know some basic facts about hiding the evidence of a crime. And I think I need to know more about my tenants up the hill."

"Seth," Meg began slowly, "maybe it's not a bad idea to try to talk to Jenn's boss at the paper."

"You know this person? Why would he talk to you, or us?"

"I think I know someone who may know him. If I say we're looking into what happened to Jenn, which happens to be true, maybe we can ask some pertinent questions. Besides, I think I could use a trip out of Granford, if only for a day. You up for it?"

"Sure. I don't have any better ideas, and it's better than going stir-crazy here."

"Tomorrow?" Meg asked.

"Works for me."

18

"You don't want to go now?" Seth asked.

"Seth, I haven't worked in Boston for over two years, and I don't know who still remembers me and can connect me with someone who matters at the paper. This newspaper is pretty high-profile, so I don't think they'd welcome a walk-in with a question about drugs and murder, without some entrée. Does that make sense?"

"Sure. How long do you think it will take?"

"Give me a couple of hours — I may have to sweet-talk some people."

"You want me to take care of getting your car window replaced?"

"Aren't you and Larry working on the tiny house today? I'd hate to take you away from that. But I love it that you asked. Even though you know full well that I can take care of the 'man stuff' myself."

"Of course I know that. I'm just trying to

use our time efficiently. I can probably give Larry some things he can finish today and set him up for tomorrow. That is, if I'm coming with you to Boston?"

"I'd like that. It's been a while since we took a road trip anywhere together. You can think about what you might like to do and see while we're there, if we have any spare time."

"I'm on it." Seth headed for his office, presumably to track down a car repair place that had a window available that would fit her middle-aged car and could be installed quickly. She stayed where she was, trying to reset her brain for Boston — who she knew, where they worked, and what approach was most likely to be successful. Then she started making a list of names.

Lauren Converse was first on her list. They'd worked together at the bank in Boston, but Lauren was the only person she would have called a friend there. They'd stayed in touch, sort of, for the first year or so after Meg had moved to Granford, but she had no idea what was going on in Lauren's life now. She could be president of the bank, or she could be selling designer handbags on Newbury Street, for all Meg knew. Still, she was a good place to start.

Meg dialed the bank's number from memory and asked for Lauren. A secretarial voice asked her for her name and then set about connecting her. Lauren picked up and started talking immediately.

"Why, if it isn't Margaret Corey! I thought you'd died or been eaten by your pigs or something."

Meg laughed. "I thought you'd be running the biggest bank in Boston by now. By the way, I'm using Chapin now. And it's goats, not pigs — I don't think goats eat people — and apples. I'm happy to say I'm surviving as a farmer, although with a minuscule profit. But I'm not calling to brag. I need your help connecting with someone."

"Gee, I don't know — what's in it for me?"

"Apart from an interesting inside story about a murder and my undying gratitude?"

"What, another murder? What is wrong with you people out there? Wasn't your mother involved in one?"

"Well, yes, but she didn't do it. And I'm not a suspect in this one, but the body was found in my backyard. Literally. By the way, this is off the record, big time."

Lauren sighed. "So I can't talk about this mysterious murder to anyone, right? Who knew that country living could be so exciting? Okay, spill it — what do you need?"

"Do you know anybody who works at the *Globe*?"

"I might. Do you mean someone who knows the dirt, or someone in power?"

"I'm not really sure who would be more useful. Let me explain. You have time?"

"I'll make time. Start talking."

Meg proceeded to outline the events that had led to her call — starting with the body in the woods, and the identification of that body that was being kept secret, and the other people nosing around Granford, and the conflict between departments at the state police, and so on. The next time she looked up, it was already dark outside and she'd been talking for over an hour.

"So, let me get this straight," Lauren said when Meg paused for breath. "The dead woman was a journalist working on a big story for the paper, but flying under the radar. She ended up dead, shot in the back, and those who know about things like that say it was murder. But they can't talk about it because the drug squad is still working their end of the case, tracking down who's who and what's what with the local drug trade that Jenn was looking into. And you're smack in the middle of it, both in location and because you take it personally and think the law enforcement people don't because they're more interested in a big score."

"That more or less covers it. And then somebody blew out my car window, while the car was in the driveway, which makes it even more personal. We think that was to make us believe that Lauren's death really was a hunting accident. They could have shot one of us if they really wanted to."

"Jeez, Meg, you make Boston sound positively safe compared to your little town. What the heck do you want from anyone at the paper?"

"Well, there's this other guy sniffing around town here but we aren't sure why. He might be picking up the pieces of the story where Jenn left off. Or he might have killed her to get her story. Or he might be part of the drug trade and wants to protect his turf. The only thing we know for sure is that he works at the paper where Jenn did — we checked their website and his picture's there. But when I talked to him, he kind of made up a story about the woman being his girlfriend and a waitress. I don't trust him, but the cops are too busy to check him out, even if they can find him."

"I get the picture. You need to talk to someone from the *Globe* who may or may not know what this Jenn person was doing out there, but who can give you the inside scoop on this Justin character. Basically, whether he's a good guy or a bad guy. So I don't think you need to talk to a senior editor — you don't happen to know who set up this investigation, do you?"

"How could I? I never met Jenn, and the only local person we know she talked to is our local homicide detective, who isn't exactly our friend."

"Oh, right. And it's possible that she originated it and took it to her bosses, rather than the other way around. Anyway, you need someone who's kind of mid-level, who knows what's coming down the pike. Are you in town now?"

"No, but we can be there any time tomorrow, if you can set something up."

"I'll get to work on it ASAP. Oh, by the way, how's married life treating you, apart from all the murders you keep tripping over?"

"It's good. We're both kind of between working seasons, but things will get busy in a month or two. Good scheduling for a murder investigation."

"It is indeed. So let me get off the phone and start working on my contacts. I'll get back to you about when and where we can meet tomorrow. And, Meg?"

"Yes?"

"Please be careful. I don't have a lot of good friends, and I can't afford to lose one."

"Got it. See you tomorrow, I hope!"

They hung up at the same time. Meg felt oddly happy: Lauren still considered her a friend, although Meg hadn't done much on her end to sustain that friendship. Funny how little she seemed to miss city living, apart from a few people like Lauren. Of course, the apple business kept her busy for most of the year. She didn't have time to miss fine restaurants or movies or plays, because she fell into bed, exhausted, almost every night. It was harder to make excuses for why she hadn't thought of heading to Boston this month, when both she and Seth had time to spare, but her head was definitely into farming, not city lights. In any event, it would be good to see Lauren, and she hoped Seth wouldn't be bored silly by their girl talk. At least he was as involved in this murder investigation as she was, and he would have different questions to ask, if they could find anyone who knew anything.

He returned victorious about half an hour later. "It's done!" he crowed.

"You are amazing. And so are your friends — unless you charmed a total stranger into doing your bidding with my poor window?"

"You're a newbie in Granford. You have to

216

have lived here most of your life to have this kind of pull."

"Then I'll let you handle that stuff. But I did my part. I talked to my banking friend Lauren, and she's going to ferret out someone at the *Globe* who knows what we need to know about Jenn and Justin. She'll call back when we have something set up."

"Aren't we efficient?" Seth said, smiling.

"That we are. I haven't seen Larry, though. Did you get a chance to talk with him?"

"I called him. He's working on the framing. I know, you can't hear him from here, but he's out there pounding away. He's really gotten into this little project. Maybe it's because it could be the first place of his own that he's ever had."

"Could be. Anyway, I should put together some questions for whoever Lauren finds who will talk to us. What do we need to know?"

Seth dropped into the chair opposite her. "Was Jenn's project common knowledge, and if so, among what group? Was it her idea or her boss's? Had she reported back to anyone or submitted a draft or notes? Then there's Justin. Were they working together? Did they have any kind of relationship? Was he jealous of her? Was he ambitious? Has anybody at the paper heard from him, or did he take vacation time? Did he ask Jenn if he could work with her, or did she recruit him to help, or was there no contact at all?"

Meg was scribbling fast. "Slow down! These are all great questions — clearly you've been thinking about all this."

"I can multitask — pound nails and think at the same time."

"I do not doubt it for a minute. Are we taking your car or mine tomorrow?"

"Do you know where we're going?"

"I know where the *Globe* building is because I worked near it, but we might be meeting our informant away from the office, so I'm not going to guess. Do we have to be back here at any particular time, or maybe I mean, do you have anything you need to do here on Saturday morning?"

"Nothing on the schedule. You thinking we should stay overnight?"

"It's worth considering. Anyway, otherwise I guess we're good to go. Maybe I should think about dinner?"

"Why are you looking like me at that? Am I supposed to go out and shoot something for dinner?"

"No, of course not. Have you eaten much wild game?"

"Only if someone else has shot it and reduced it to recognizable cuts of meat. I've had venison sausage, venison burgers, and probably a few other things I haven't noticed. You?"

"I've eaten rabbit a few times. Physically it looks a lot like chicken, which I eat without protest, but I've had a lot of stuffed bunnies in my life, so I always feel guilty. Should we not eat cute food?"

"That's your personal choice. I don't want to give up animal protein, but I don't feel strongly either way."

"Good to know. I think we're having lamb stew for dinner, if I ever get it started."

Meg had assembled all the components for the stew in a large enameled casserole and was sliding it into the oven, set on low, when Lauren finally called. When Meg picked up, Lauren said, "Got him! Junior reporter but he's worked at the paper for a few years, and his desk is in the bullpen near Jenn's. So he overheard some cryptic conversations, but he's smart enough to put together the pieces. Does that work for you?"

"Sounds great. Lunch?"

"I'll give you a call and tell you where we can meet. Do I get to sit in?"

"As long as you can keep your mouth

shut. The state police on our end won't be happy if all this gets out before they say we can talk. I'm surprised we haven't seen reporters crawling around our property already. I guess that means the state police are doing a good job of being mysterious — you know, unidentified body found in uncleared part of town, period."

"Ooh, cloak-and-dagger stuff. Great! Talk in the morning tomorrow."

After Meg hung up, she turned to Seth. "Well, we're set. Should we tell Art?"

"That's hard to say," Seth answered. "We're not conducting an official interview — this is off the record. You did tell Lauren that this still wasn't public knowledge." When Meg nodded, Seth went on, "We know the state homicide unit is muzzled until the narcotics unit gets whatever they're looking for, so nobody officially knows it was Jenn who died, so nobody has made a connection to the *Globe* or even to Boston, except that one guy who came here looking for her, who was probably Justin. Odd, isn't it, that you and I know more about this murder than most of the people in town? Or even beyond?"

"It is indeed. I told Lauren this whole thing was being downplayed. I can understand why, but when someone shoots at my car, I can't just sit back and ignore it. So we go to Boston and we ask questions, and if anybody asks what we were doing in Boston, we say we were having lunch with an old friend and colleague of mine, and she happened to bring along a friend. End of story?"

"Works for me. And let's leave Art out of this for the moment. Then he can plead ignorance without lying."

19

The weather kindly cooperated with their planned excursion: no snow or ice. Meg agonized about whether to wear fashionable shoes (if she could find any in her closet) or comfortable ones and decided in favor of the latter. If Seth was willing, she would be happy to park the car somewhere and ramble around the city that had once been her home, what seemed like a few thousand years ago. And she was excited about seeing Lauren and catching up, and looking forward to playing sleuth to get the inside story on Jenn's murder, if possible. Okay, that was a bit silly of her — did she really think she was Nancy Drew? — and might even be illegal, if the state police in Northampton decided that she and Seth were interfering with a police investigation. She didn't think she was interfering — she was just nudging the process along, which she felt she had the right to do. The drug people could focus on their drug investigation — she'd be happy to stay as far away as possible from that. She just wanted to know why Jenn had been dumped on her property.

They set off for Boston after breakfast. Seth drove and wound his way easily into the city. "You've done this before, haven't you?" Meg commented.

"Did you really think I was a country bumpkin?" he replied, his gaze not leaving the maze of Boston streets. "The only problem is when they move roads and access ramps around, which they seem to do regularly around here."

"I hear you. I rarely drove in the city when I worked here. In nice weather I would walk, and in lousy weather I'd take the T."

"You heard from Lauren yet?" he asked.

"No, but we're early. Any sightseeing you want to do? Museums? Historic sites?"

"I don't think we have time to do justice to a museum, although I'll admit I'd like to see what they've done with the Gardner since the last time I was here. As for historic locations, I've probably seen a lot of those over the years. A nice cemetery, maybe?"

"Looking for relatives or heroes?"

"No relatives, but there are a lot of big names buried in the one across from the Parker House. Old Granary. I always like to say hello to Paul Revere and Sam Adams."

"Sir, you have hidden depths. So why don't we park around there somewhere and walk?"

"Sounds good."

As they emerged from the parking garage under the Boston Common, Meg's phone rang, and she answered quickly. "Hey, Lauren. We still on?"

"We are. Where are you?"

"We just parked under the Common. We were going to play tourist."

"How about we meet at the Parker House at noon?"

"You read my mind. Seth wants to visit the cemetery across the street. Is our contact still on board?"

"When I said I'd pay for lunch he jumped at the chance. I'll book a table — a quiet one — and you can look like clueless tourists while we all talk."

"Great. See you at noon then."

Meg turned to Seth after she hung up. "I love it when a plan comes together. Parker House at noon. What do you want to see between now and then?"

They strolled aimlessly, admiring the venerable architecture surrounding the Common (with a number of much more recent additions), noting changes unfamiliar to them, moving just fast enough to keep warm. "This is nice," Meg said after a while. "We should do this more often."

"I agree. Providence isn't too far. Or Newport. In easy reach."

"Either sounds great to me. Should we head for the restaurant now?"

"I suppose. The cemetery should keep until after we eat."

Lauren was already waiting when they walked into the lobby, and standing next to her was a casually dressed man about their own age. Meg and Lauren hugged enthusiastically, ignoring the embarrassed looks of their companions. Lauren introduced them to the other man. "Toby, this is Meg, formerly Corey, currently Chapin — she was the only other sane person at the bank when we were both there."

"Are things any better now?" Meg felt compelled to ask, smiling.

"Not really. And this is Seth Chapin, her shiny new husband of — what is it, three months? These two went all country on me — Meg now grows apples, and Seth saves crumbling old houses."

"Good to meet you both," Toby said. "At least you can eat your output, Meg, which is more than many people can say."

"I'm still learning how to grow apples —

it's definitely more challenging than crunching numbers."

"Shall we find our table?" Lauren asked. "I requested one in the corner. I said you were from out of town *and* newlyweds, and I was afraid you might be noisy."

"Gee, thanks, Lauren," Meg said.

They fell silent while the hostess escorted them to their seats and retreated after handing them menus. "Oh, sweetie, we have to have the Boston cream pie! They're famous for it!" Meg said to Seth in a louder-than-usual high-pitched voice.

"Sure, pumpkin, that sounds great," Seth replied in the same spirit.

Lauren and Toby were staring at them as though they'd grown horns. "Hey, we were just trying to establish our characters," Meg protested.

"Consider your job done," Lauren said sternly. "Now, let's order so we can get down to business."

"I'm having the New England clam chowder and the New England lobster roll. And the Boston cream pie, of course. What?" she exclaimed when Seth stared at her. "I don't get out of Granford enough, so I'm making up for it. You can have whatever you like."

Orders placed, accompanied by iced tea so they could all keep their heads clear, Meg leaned forward and lowered her voice. "Lauren, how much have you told Toby? Or maybe I should be asking, how much does or did Toby know?"

"Hey, I'm right here. I knew Jenn pretty well," Toby spoke up quickly. "She is, uh, was a few years older than me, but we kind of came up together, and hung out after work. Is she really . . . ?"

"I'm afraid so, but don't spread that around, even at the paper. It's a complicated situation." Meg proceeded to repeat the now-familiar story, carefully tailored to avoid attracting any attention from adjoining tables, with Seth contributing details occasionally. Finally she said, "We're not here on behalf of any law enforcement agency, but I feel like I have a stake in the outcome, which I think you can understand. There are a lot of people inside the investigation pulling in different directions, and I don't think that's helping. Actually, the more I think about it, the more curious I get about Justin, and where he fits in all this. Can you shed any light on that, Toby?"

Toby thought for a moment before replying. "Maybe I should take a step back and tell you my impression of Jenn. She was one damn fine reporter. She worked hard, she checked her sources, and she had a strong sense of priorities. She was also willing to help anyone who was struggling, which included me when I joined the paper. An all-around good person. Once she got hold of an idea, she was absolutely dogged about pursuing it, although this last effort of hers went far beyond anything she'd done before. But she wasn't reckless — she believed she was ready to take it on, and I wouldn't disagree."

"Did she tell you anything about what she was doing?"

"Only bits and pieces. It wasn't that she didn't trust me, but she figured the fewer people who knew what she was doing and where she was going to be, the better for everyone. She believed she had ahold of something big, but she also knew it could be dangerous. I've assumed she told her plans to at least one of the senior editors, but nobody talked about it in-house."

"And Justin?"

Toby's expression changed to carefully neutral. "He was kind of the new kid on the block, newer than even me. I don't kid myself — I'm not high on the pecking order, but neither am I at the bottom. I work hard too, and I'm learning all the time. I deliver on time, and my copy is clean. I was hoping to be another Jenn in a couple more years."

Toby took a swig of his iced tea. "I don't know where Justin came from — if I had to guess I'd say he was someone's pet nephew. He was ambitious from the start, and he didn't seem to care who he stepped on to get what he wanted. He watched Jenn like a hawk."

"Were they involved personally?"

"Very unlikely. She saw right through him, which pissed him off. But like I said, he watched her, and I'd guess that he overheard enough to figure out what she was working on. Not the details, but the general outline. You know, big story, very hush-hush. That made him sit up and pay attention."

"So how did she go after her story?" Seth asked. "She must have been absent from the paper for at least a week or two, working her way into whatever was happening in our part of the state. How did anyone explain that?"

Toby made air quotes. "On assignment. No further explanation."

"And nobody made the connection with the unidentified woman found in Granford?"

"To be best of my knowledge, no one did or has since. The people on your end kept it very quiet. There's still no official ID. And of course, none of our people were looking

229

in that direction. Except Justin, apparently."

"We have heard," Meg said cautiously, "that he was seen in our town before her death. So he must have figured something out."

"Jenn was careful, but it's possible she left some scribbled message that gave him enough to work with. Or hell, maybe he had contacts of his own and figured things out that way. He never asked me where she was."

Meg thought hard before phrasing her next question. "How far would he have gone to get a big story?"

Toby stared at Meg. "You mean, would he have killed her? I doubt it — I don't think he had the guts to do that. But he might have deliberately blown her cover to the wrong people somehow."

Seth said grimly, "He would do that? That's pretty risky."

"Wouldn't surprise me, and I bet he'd have kept his hands clean," Toby said. "Once she was out of the way he'd have the inside track on the story. Not a pretty picture, is it? I wish I had anything like proof to give you, but most of us are focused mainly on what goes on in Boston. I don't think we look past Worcester."

"Do you have any reason to believe that

what Jenn was into in our area has ties to anything going on in this end of the state?" Seth asked.

"Not a clue. From things I've read, I gather your neighborhood is the new hot territory, with all those college kids around, not to mention faculty and tourists, but it would be easier to get product from New Hampshire, where things are pretty loose. But I'm just guessing. Sorry — I really liked Jenn, and I wish I could do more to help."

Meg glanced around the table. "If — a big if — we find out what happened, and if Jenn left any materials behind — notes, emails, whatever — would you want to take over the story?"

"Sure, as long as Justin is out of the way — I mean, legally. I admit it, I'm ambitious, but not at anyone else's expense. But I think Jenn deserves recognition for what she did, if there's anything to show for it."

Meg and Seth exchanged a glance. "I think that about covers our questions. Is Justin still hanging around the paper? Or did he take a sudden vacation or catch an unexpected flu?"

"He's been in and out, but unpredictably. You said you've seen him?"

"Heck, I talked to him and gave him coffee," Meg said, trying to keep the anger out of her voice. "And listened to him lie to my face, when I knew what the truth was. And I just smiled and played dumb. I suppose he could claim he had made up a cover story, but I'm not convinced. And then we learned that he'd been seen in our neighborhood *before* Jenn's body was found. We live in farm country, so there's not much reason for him to have been there."

"Maybe he needed an inconspicuous place to crash?" Toby suggested.

"Could be. And then he did start asking around town if anyone had seen his girlfriend Jenn. I couldn't swear when that was in relation to when we knew she was dead. There just isn't a lot to go on, but I know I didn't trust him."

Toby glanced suddenly at his watch. "Shoot, I've got a deadline and I'd better go. Meg, Seth, thank you for sharing this information. I won't tell anyone else until you give me the go-ahead. I hope I've helped. I'm truly sorry about what happened to Jenn, and if there's anything I can do — a bit late — just ask."

"Can I ask you to steer clear of Justin until we fit together a few more pieces?" Seth said. "He may still think he's safe."

"Sure. Loose lips and all that. And if and when you give me the go-ahead, I'll see if anybody else at the paper wants in on the story. Jenn was popular, and she'll be missed." Toby stopped to fish a slightly bent business card from his pocket. "You can reach me here. You do email?"

"Uh, yes, Toby," Meg said sarcastically. "We may be hicks, but we do use computers."

"Sorry," Toby said. He grinned, which made him look even younger. "Hope I'll be hearing from you. Bye, Lauren — thanks for inviting me." He held up a hand in farewell, then walked across the large room toward the exit.

When he'd gone through the doors, Meg said to Lauren, "You were very quiet."

"I didn't know Jenn, and I don't know squat about drug dealers, thank goodness. Did you get what you wanted from Toby?"

"Definitely. And thank you for setting that up. He was exactly the kind of insider we needed to talk with. If there's any way we can feed him the story, I'd be happy to. As long as it doesn't get us arrested."

"Any idea when the state police are going to wrap things up?" Lauren asked.

"Not a clue," Meg told her. "They won't even talk to the head homicide detective, who sometimes talks to our local police chief, who has no trouble telling us anything he knows because he knows we won't spread it around. So bottom line, don't hold your breath."

"Got it. You heading home today?"

Meg looked at Seth once again before answering Lauren. "I guess so. I'm sorry I haven't been a better friend to you. I owe you one."

"You mean, like forgetting I exist for months at a time? That's okay — I understand. New job, new husband. You'll get over it, and when you do, I'll be waiting. On the other hand, if you're dead, please let me know."

"Of course. Hold a séance with Toby and I'll explain everything after the fact."

"Perfect. Now, can we enjoy this great food?"

They ate while discussing ordinary matters that didn't include murder, and Meg enjoyed every bite. Finally, as she scraped the last remnants of Boston cream pie off her plate, she said, "That really was wonderful. Seth, we should do this more often. Maybe twice a year?"

"Or you could invite Lauren out to our neck of the woods for a pastoral weekend, and prove that we have good restaurants too."

"I'll take it," Lauren said quickly.

They all stood up. "Seth, you still want to say hi to John Hancock?" Meg asked.

"It's a tradition of mine. Won't take a minute."

"Both of you, go!" Lauren said. "At least the traffic should be light. Come here, you." Lauren grabbed Meg in a fierce hug. "Take care of yourself."

"Thank you, Lauren — for everything."

20

They parted ways with Lauren on the sidewalk in front of the hotel, and Meg followed Seth across the busy street and into the cemetery opposite. Seth seemed to know exactly where he was going, so Meg just followed him. "That's Paul Revere there," Seth said, pointing. "Sam Adams is over there." He pointed again.

"Boston must have been a very different place in their day."

"Yes and no, I guess," Seth replied. "But it's worth it to me to come here and honor their memories, and what they did. Which has survived, in a variety of ways, until this day." He made one more full turn, scanning the tombstones, then said, "Ready to go?"

"I'd rather get home before it's fully dark. Do you mind?"

"Of course not. There's commuter traffic to consider too. We can go — and we can come back again if we want."

"There is that," Meg agreed.

Fifteen minutes later they had extricated the car from the parking garage and were pointed in the right direction, although no one would say they were moving fast. "Now I remember why I don't like cities," Seth said as another car with out-of-town plates cut him off at a corner.

"I do know what you mean."

Meg let Seth concentrate on his driving, remaining silent until they had reached the Massachusetts Turnpike in Weston and could move more quickly. Seth relaxed perceptibly as the road before him opened up. "What have we learned?" he asked.

"From Toby? Well, he more or less confirmed my impression of Justin — he's an opportunist, and he's up to something, although it's not clear what."

"Do you think he's a threat? Or just over-reaching?"

"I don't really know. A threat to what? Us? The investigation? Clearly he knew Jenn, but would he have killed her for a story? It's hard for me to read somebody based on one encounter, but Toby didn't think so. I might call Justin manipulative, and a little arrogant. Full of himself."

"Why arrogant?"

"Because he thought it would be easy to

fool me, that he could get by on charm and good looks, but he was careless."

"Hmm." Seth drove a couple of miles in silence, then said, "Meg, what do you think is going on? And where does Justin fit? It's been over a week now, with no apparent results. Even the drug police can't let this drag on much longer without making a lot of people look stupid or incompetent."

"I agree a hundred percent. How could they not know anything by now? But big picture? Much as I hate to say it, I think there are drugs in Granford, being sold in town and beyond. I don't know anything about how much money is involved, and how much trade it would take to make it a big operation. Could be it's just a toehold, in a nice quiet community where nobody is looking for such a thing, but it could grow. Maybe that's why the state police drug unit is so anxious to keep what they're doing under wraps — they'd like to nip it in the bud. Without outside interference from people like us."

"Maybe. So Jenn was a threat to their effort?"

"Maybe. She may have cleared it with narcotics, but it could be she got too involved with the story and went too far. It's hard to say without knowing the woman."

"If the narcotics squad or whatever they are won't talk to Marcus, who at least is playing on the same team, they probably didn't say much to a journalist from Boston. Unless she had some prior connection to someone? But how do you call up someone in that group and say, 'Hello, did you ever talk to Jenn Chambers about your current investigation?' I'm sure they'd answer if I asked nicely."

"Meg, you definitely sound frustrated."

"Shouldn't I? There are a lot of people who have some information, but nobody's willing to share. I don't expect them to provide this information to just anybody. Why should they? But I'm not just anybody. I have a track record with the police — they can ask Marcus. Oh, that's right, they don't talk to him either. But I did have a body in the backyard, so that should give me some privileges."

"There is that," Seth admitted. "The whole idea of drugs in Granford troubles me. As a community leader, I should know about it. But I have no idea what I'm looking for, and every time I try to picture it, I come up with bad stereotypes of outsiders lurking in corners and handing out packets of something or other, when they aren't shooting at each other in some turf war the rest of us can't begin to understand."

"I know. But from what little I've read or seen on the news, things are a lot more white-collar than they used to be, which makes them less noticeable. You and I have probably had nice ordinary conversations with some of these people without even noticing. I'm beginning to feel like a naïve dinosaur."

"Interesting image, but I know what you mean. All this drug stuff boiled up over the past few years, while we weren't looking. So what now?"

Meg watched the wintry landscape roll by for a while. Finally she said, "Seth, Larry made a comment the other day about how much coming and going there is up at the house. Not him, obviously, but the other guys there."

"So? Should that mean something?" Seth asked.

"Hear me out. Larry thought they were partying with friends, so he hid in his room and tried to shut out the noise. If that's true, he wouldn't know what they were doing. But he implied — and I'd want to check with him — that it went on a lot of the time, not just Saturday nights. So tell me: if you were a drug dealer, handling pretty clean stuff, how would you get it into the hands of your customers? You can't exactly advertise or put up signs. And you can't hang around on street corners in Noho or Amherst for long without somebody in law enforcement noticing. Maybe not right away, but if they're doing their jobs I don't think it would take long."

"Are you going somewhere with this?"

"Yes, I think so. Say they want to set up a semi-permanent base somewhere that's not quite as obvious as the center of one town or another, but not too far out to discourage customers. Wouldn't an isolated old house in Granford be a good place to do business?"

"And you're saying you think that's what all the traffic is about?"

"It's possible, isn't it? Somebody would have to keep track of who was coming and going — like the same people, or different people each time — but people would have a good excuse. "Oh, I guess I'm lost — I'd heard there was a party out this way." And if they're selling illegal prescription drugs, they would be really easy to conceal. You think drug-sniffing dogs could find them?"

"Meg, I can't guess. So you're saying you think one or more of the three guys who aren't Larry are running a drug operation out of my house, and none of us noticed?"

"It's possible, isn't it? It's not something we'd be on the lookout for. Like Larry, we'd figure it was just a bunch of young guys leading a normal college life and partying a lot."

"And we have absolutely zero evidence for any sort of activity like this, apart from Larry's word," Seth pointed out. "Plus, if they are selling pills, that wouldn't generate much trash, and it would be easy to hide."

"You do have the right to inspect the house — it's yours, isn't it?"

"Yes, but I'd feel awkward barging in and telling whoever's home that I needed to check if the plumbing was leaking."

"That kind of raises another point. Is there always someone there, who could be taking care of business? Or are there times when the house is empty and you could go in?"

"Meg, this whole thing is like a house of cards. You're suggesting that a couple or three kids are running a drug operation up the hill from us, which may or may not be large but was apparently important enough for someone to kill a snoopy reporter."

"Yes, I guess that's what I'm saying. You have any better ideas?"

"Not specifically. We can run it by Art, and I suppose I could give him permission to search the place legally, but if he does that and comes up empty we will have upended the drug unit's operation, and I don't think they'll be very happy about that."

"What can they do to us?"

"We will have interfered with a police investigation based solely on a paranoid hunch. I'm sure there's a crime in there somewhere. And I'm just about as sure that Art will catch some flack too."

"Can we talk with Art?"

"Maybe. But if he officially knows what we believe, he might be liable if he doesn't act on it."

"Maybe he already knows and hasn't told us? To protect us?" Meg suggested hopefully.

"Meg, I simply don't know. I'm out of my depth here, and I suspect you are too. The problem is, we can come up with as many pretty theories as we want, but we can't prove anything, and we risk doing harm to a variety of people — not just ourselves, but my mother and Christopher. And Larry."

"So we just sit around and wring our hands and complain? Behind closed windows and locked doors? Is that what you want life in Granford to be like?"

"I didn't say that, Meg. But we need to

243

find out as much as possible before we do anything — *if* we do anything."

Meg swallowed a sharp reply. Seth was right: there was no good reason to go charging into this blindly, no matter how strongly she felt. But how were they going to get more information if no one was willing to talk? Including the authorities? She stayed silent for the rest of the trip back.

It was already dark when they pulled into their driveway. Meg briefly entertained visions of a charred hulk of a house — torched in order to silence them. Or a mangled corpse of an animal, its throat slashed, deposited outside the door. *Get a grip, Meg!* she told herself. If — still an if — there was drug activity in the town, the dealers' goal should be to keep a low profile so they could stay in business, not call attention to themselves. Perversely that made her and Seth safer.

They'd barely gotten inside and fed the animals when the phone rang. Seth answered. "Oh, hi, Mom. No, we haven't eaten dinner — we made a very fast trip to Boston and we just got back. Sure, that sounds good. See you in five."

"Let me guess: your mother just invited us to dinner," Meg said with a half smile.

"Got it in one. You okay with that?"

"Sure. I don't feel like cooking anyway, and we should fill Lydia in about what's happened since we last saw her. Will Christopher be there?"

"I didn't ask, but probably. You ready to go?"

"I'll just put my coat back on."

After a brief debate about walking versus driving the half mile or so to Lydia's house, they decided to take the car. The ride took them all of two minutes. Lydia greeted them happily at the door, and as Seth had predicted, Christopher was hovering in the background. "Something smells wonderful," Meg said as Seth helped her off with her coat.

"Corned beef and cabbage," Lydia said. "I felt like cooking today, and there's no point in making the dish for only two people, so I got carried away. How was Boston?"

"Good," Meg said. "We had lunch with an old friend of mine at the Parker House."

"Oh, dear," Lydia said. "That may be hard to compete with."

"Hey, we're happy to be here, Mom," Seth said. "Good company. Although Meg and I did decide we should get out of Granford more than we have lately. Maybe the four of us could plan a short trip, although between

245

the orchard, renovation season and the academic calendar, it would take some planning."

"But it's worth considering," Christopher said firmly.

"Are you two ready to eat, after your elegant lunch?" Lydia asked.

"More like ready to crash early," Meg told her. "It's been a long and busy day. I apologize in advance if we're not sparkling company tonight."

"You get a free pass," Lydia said. "You're family."

The food was good, the conversation flowed easily, but in spite of that Meg felt her eyelids drooping, and it wasn't even nine o'clock. She really had turned into a farmer, keeping farmers' hours — up with the sun, in bed by dark.

She snapped back to attention when Christopher said to Seth, "There's been a lot of comings and goings at your house, Seth."

"Really?" he replied. "I can't see it from our place, but Larry said the other guys like to party."

"I do dimly recall being young," Lydia said, smiling, "but I didn't realize that today's young people partied around the clock."

"What do you mean?" Seth asked.

"There are vehicles coming and going much of the night," Christopher said.

"The headlights shine on our house, when they turn into the driveway," Lydia added. "We never used to notice that."

"The odd thing is that the comings and goings seem to go on all day as well," Christopher noted. "You know about Larry's whereabouts, but it strikes me as surprising that three other young men would generate so much traffic."

That was odd, Meg agreed silently. And then she stilled, trying to drag out a nagging thought. "How much has Seth told you about the murdered woman?"

"That she was a journalist," Lydia replied, "and she was here working on a story about drugs. I know, we're supposed to keep this quiet, but we haven't talked with anyone except you two about it. Why do you ask?"

"Because now we're wondering whether the other boys — or men — are doing something other than having a good time over there. If there's that much new traffic, and many of the cars don't stay long, is it possible that they're picking up drugs? That one or more of the guys is a dealer?"

21

Lydia looked startled. "Why on earth would you say that, Meg?"

"Well, you know it was the state police narcotics unit that clamped down on giving out any information about the death, right?"

"That's what you told us. What did you think that meant?"

Seth picked up the thread. "That they believed there was something involving drugs going on locally and they had some sort of grand plan in place to shut it down, and they didn't want anything reported on the news to mess that up. Jenn talked to the narcotics people about a big story covering the surge in drug activity in this area, and that was why she was here."

"But she never told Art," Meg said, "although that might have made sense. She'd already talked with the narcotics unit, at the beginning, but maybe they believed she wouldn't find what she was looking for, or maybe they just blew her off. But she didn't stop digging. That's why Seth and I were in Boston today — we needed to talk to someone at the paper who knew her and see if that person might have known what Jenn was doing. And if he did know, did he think that she had shared that information with anyone at the paper." *Like Justin.*

"And?" Lydia asked.

Meg answered. "Toby, the reporter we met with — off the record — said he sat near Jenn's desk and picked up enough by eavesdropping to figure out she had something big in her sights, but he didn't pass that on to anyone. He also figured her editor had to know something."

"So why is the poor woman dead?" Lydia asked. "If only a very few people knew what she was doing here."

"That we still don't know," Meg said. "And we don't know why she was dumped where she was. If I'd been the killer, I would have made sure she was found nowhere near my home base. Like in the river, or along the highway fifty miles from here. Seth and I guessed that maybe the killer was interrupted, or he was in too much of a hurry. Or he was an idiot, not to mention careless. Or I suppose he might have been sending a signal to any competitors."

"What kind of drugs do you think they're selling?" Lydia asked tentatively.

Seth answered that question. "Mom, Meg and I are babes in the woods when it comes to what's popular in drugs," he said. "The only name I've heard kicked around is fentanyl, and all I know about it is what I read online. It is fairly easy to make, it's very strong, and it can be deadly. Once you're hooked, withdrawal is really hard. And law enforcement is scrambling to keep up with it. It's the single biggest cause of the current opioid epidemic. Which is very real in the Pioneer Valley, and growing fast."

"You're saying that they may be making this awful stuff next door?" Christopher asked, incredulous.

"It's possible," Seth told him. "I don't know all the details of production or what kind of equipment and supplies you would need, but there's space in and outside the house, and I'm sure that would be plenty large enough to make enough of the stuff for local distribution. But that assumes that the owner — that would be me — wouldn't be dropping by regularly just to chat and might see what they were doing. It also assumes that everyone at the house had to be involved or at least aware of what was going on there. I think it's more likely that they would have taken an easier route and found a supplier somewhere else, who delivers the goods ready to sell. In which case they're just distributing it, not making it themselves. But based on what you tell us about all the comings and goings, they're doing a lot of business. Still, I don't think the narcotics unit in Northampton would be eager to explain it all to us."

"Seth," Meg interrupted, "you know we still have no evidence that this is what's going on next door — only an increase in daily car traffic, which is not exactly conclusive. The state police would probably laugh at us if we told them what we suspect, whether or not it's true. I suppose it's possible that they might not have observed that particular fact, but they might laugh at us anyway just to throw us off. Their message for us — and even Marcus and Art — is loud and clear: butt out. But I'd guess the stakes are pretty high. I'm sure they'd rather not let it spread in the area and become a much bigger problem. And those guys at the house have had, what, only a couple of months to get established? They should be stopped before they become a neighborhood fixture."

"Assuming you're correct, what should we do now?" Christopher asked.

"I wish I knew," Seth told him. "It's clear

none of us is happy with doing nothing, but we don't want to find ourselves in the middle of a major police operation. Meg pointed out that it's my house and therefore I have every right to go in and check things out, but I'm not sure it's ever completely empty, and I'd hate to go searching around poking through things, even though I am the owner."

"Seth, that might even be dangerous," Meg protested, "if you startled one or another of them. We believe they've already killed one person. And they might even make the case that they thought you were an intruder, if you go barging in unannounced."

Seth shrugged, looking uncomfortable.

"Seth, are you thinking that more than one of the lads in involved with this?" Christopher asked.

"I really don't know, Christopher. Maybe three of them. I don't think Larry is part of this, but he hasn't said much, beyond that he tries to shut himself in his room and ignore whatever is going on. Nor have we asked him. But selling drugs does not fit with his character."

"Have you considered that he might have good reason to remain silent?" Christopher said carefully.

"What do you mean?" Meg asked. Larry was, after all, her employee, and if there was a problem that involved Larry, she should know about it.

"Under normal circumstances I would not share this information, but things are hardly normal now, are they?" Christopher began. "I recommended him to work with you after Bree left, Meg, and I have every faith in his capabilities and firsthand knowledge of growing apples. But I don't know whether he's talked to you about his own background, which is less than conventional."

"It's clear he has relevant orchard experience," Meg acknowledged, "but you'd already told me that. He seldom shares any personal information. What else should I know?"

"His childhood was, you might say, unsettled. His family owned a small farm, which produced barely enough to turn a profit, even in the best of years. From what little he's shared with me, he did most of the work on the place to keep it going. His father was a heavy drinker, who turned to drugs in his later years, while Larry was still living there. The father was, you might say, known to the police in the area, although I gather he was never convicted of any major crime."

"What does that have to do with Larry?"

Christopher cleared his throat. "Rightly or wrongly, Larry might fear that he would be tarred with the same brush as his father, which means he might well have turned a blind eye to illicit activities in your house, Seth. He was in a difficult position. He is committed to working for you, Meg, and helping you improve your orchard, but I would guess that he would rather not make a fuss about something if he's not quite sure it of yet — the drug business. Plus, he no doubt assumes that the police would see him as the most likely suspect, perhaps without regard to any real evidence and based solely on his family history. Maintaining ignorance may have seemed the best compromise, from his perspective."

Meg chose her next words carefully. "Do you think he was aware of these possible activities before Jenn's death?"

"That I cannot say," Christopher said. "He does not confide in me, and what I've said is mostly inference. I cannot tell you whether Larry ever crossed paths with her, much less whether he knows who her killer was. I'm inclined to think not, because I believe he has a moral line that he will not cross, and killing someone, particularly a woman, falls beyond that line. Drugs he knows and understands to a degree, but murder is an entirely different category."

"I'd certainly like to think so," Meg said firmly. "He's got some native smarts, so it does seem unlikely that he hasn't noticed anything odd going on at the house, but I can see the dilemma he faces. I wonder if his interest in building the tiny house is something he sees as a way to get out of the house without offending anyone, including you, Seth."

"But would he ignore Jenn's murder? And what about the bullet shot at your car?" Seth demanded.

"What?" Lydia exclaimed. "Someone shot at you?"

"I'm sorry, Lydia, I thought we'd already told you. This is getting so complicated!" Meg exclaimed.

"I'll give you the quick version," Seth told his mother. "Someone shot out the passenger-side window of Meg's car while it was parked in the driveway. We were inside the house. It appears that the bullet came from roughly the same location where Jenn's body was found. But before you overreact, Art thought that the shot was meant to do noticeable damage but not hurt anyone. Again, a possible warning, and one that could be passed off as a misfire by an inept hunter. I think the shooter, whoever it was, wanted to reinforce the myth of the hunter, which would in turn reinforce the theory about how Jenn died. But since we know too much, among us, that didn't exactly work — that shot made it more likely that Jenn's shooting was deliberate, as was where she was placed."

"Seth, I'm so sorry," Lydia said.

"Why?"

"Because all this has nothing to do with you! All you did was rent out your house at a low rate, to help people out. They weren't supposed to start killing people and shooting at you."

"Mom, you're getting way ahead of your facts. All this is theory. Maybe they're all just ordinary rowdy twenty-somethings and this blossoming drug business in our backyard is all a fantasy."

"Seth, we're ignoring the obvious. We could just ask Larry," Meg countered.

Everyone stared at her.

"Well," she began defensively, "how else are we going to find out how much he knows? Look, I haven't pried into his history because I respect his privacy — he's my employee, not a friend. But circumstances have changed. I wouldn't want us to gang up on him as a group, because I'm pretty sure that would spook him, and we wouldn't get anything out of him. He works for me, so I should be the one to talk to him."

"My dear, I was the one who recommended him to you," Christopher pointed out. "I feel a certain responsibility, to him and of course to you."

"And I appreciate that, Christopher," Meg told him. "But I don't want him to retreat like a snail into his shell and then disappear into the night, with none of this resolved. I don't believe he's done anything wrong, except maybe by omission, by not sharing any suspicions he might have. He may know something about drugs or Jenn's death or he may not, but I won't believe he'd stand by and do nothing if Seth or I, and by extension you two, were at risk."

"And exactly what would you be asking him?" Seth demanded, his tone angry.

Meg turned to face him. "If he had noticed any suspicious activity among his housemates. If he suspected any kind of illegal activity. If he had overheard anything at the house that troubled him. If he knows what happened to Jenn, and if any of the other people in his house had anything to do with it. And if he trusts us enough to do the right thing, and not just throw him under the bus."

"Well, that about sums it up," Seth said.

Meg stared at him. "Are you being sarcastic?"

"Actually, yes," he said. "This is ridiculous. We have a more than adequate police force only a couple of towns over, and we know they're looking at all this. Are they stupid? Incompetent? Can't you see why they would resent a pack of rank amateurs getting in the way of their investigation?"

"But we have information that they need to know!" Meg protested.

"Why do you assume they don't already know what we know?" Seth shot back. "Just because they aren't moving fast enough to make you happy doesn't mean they aren't all over this. We get caught in the crossfire, one or more of us could get hurt. What if instead of blowing out your car window they decide to go after the goats? Or Max? Or one of us?"

A thick silence fell as each of them contemplated the possible consequences. Finally Lydia said, "Shouldn't you at least ask Art for help, Seth?"

"Mom, we've kept him in the loop from the beginning, but he's getting shut out at the other end, and to be fair, investigating a homicide is not his responsibility. The staties think he's only a local cop — what could he know?"

"And Detective Marcus? He is, after all, a homicide detective," Christopher pointed out.

"Same story," Seth said. "The narcotics unit is hogging the show. I suppose they have every right to worry about leaks. And if our neighbors here don't have any big investment in equipment or production, they can pick up and move pretty fast, if they think someone has figured out what they're doing. Look, I'll take some responsibility for this mess. I didn't really think it through. The house was sitting empty, and I knew there were people around who'd like an affordable place to live. I didn't exactly do any research on their backgrounds. I just took it on faith that anybody who applied for a room this far from the colleges and jobs couldn't exactly be troublemakers. Okay, I was naïve."

"Did they apply as a group?" Meg asked suddenly. "Apart from Larry, I mean?"

"Maybe. I think it was sort of an 'I know another guy who's looking' and I ended up with the three of them. But they didn't actually present themselves as a group. And we still don't know if they're all involved — if there's anything to be involved in. We may have blown all this out of proportion. Or we've all developed an inflated sense of paranoia and we're seeing bogeymen behind every bush."

"But Jenn is dead," Meg said quietly. "And the evidence suggests it wasn't a simple accident."

"And we may never know who was responsible," Seth replied.

"And this problem will all just go away?" Meg protested.

"Or the state police will make a big drug bust and it'll be all over the news for two days, and then life in sleepy Granford will go back to normal. Minus drug dealers."

"Do you really believe that, Seth?"

Seth sighed. "No, Meg, I don't. Not in my gut." He looked at the people around the table, one at a time. "Look, it's been a long day for us, and now is not the time to make any decisions. Let's sleep on it and get together tomorrow. Keep your eyes open, but don't do anything. We're playing with fire here."

"It's hard to believe," Lydia said, shaking her head. "I've lived in this house for some forty years, and I never expected to encounter something like this. It makes me sad."

"I know. But we'll see what we can do about it. In the morning."

22

Meg and Seth didn't say much on the short drive back to their house. Once home, they went about their chores equally silently: feeding the pets, walking Max, checking that doors were locked. Once that was accomplished, they found themselves in the kitchen. Too late in the evening for coffee, and neither of them felt like an alcoholic nightcap.

"What happened, Seth?" Meg finally said. "A week ago life was normal, happy, productive. Now suddenly we've found ourselves in the middle of a drug-dealing operation with a body in our backyard. What went wrong?"

"Meg, I think it's been happening for a long time, out there in the rest of the state, or even the country. Granford was lucky because we got ignored — we were too small and unimportant to bother with. Now the whole marketing angle for drugs has gotten more strategic. When most people hear 'drugs' they think of gangs and big cities, not quiet rural towns. But the market is here, and people know that now. And the drugs are easier to transport and sell. We — you and I, and most of the people around here — just didn't notice the changes."

"And we can't reverse it, can we." Meg made it a statement rather than a question.

"I don't think so. Come here."

Meg walked into his arms and they leaned into each other, wordlessly. Finally she said, "But can't we do something about our little corner, or is it already too late?"

"Meg, I really don't know. Now that our eyes are opened, we're going to have to think about it. Please, don't do anything rash."

"Like what? Walk into your house up the hill with a loaded shotgun and blow the baddies away?"

"That's not the right way to do it, and you know it."

"Yes, I do. But I want to feel that I'm doing *something*. Poor Jenn — that was probably all she wanted, to reveal the problem and maybe inspire people to pay attention and do something about it, although maybe with a dash of power and glory and public recognition for her. But she risked her life to get her story, and look how she ended up. How are we supposed to fight this?"

"I don't have an easy answer, Meg. Carefully, I hope."

"I'm going to talk to Larry. One on one." Seth backed away from their embrace. "Are you sure that's a good idea?"

"Heck, I'm not sure of anything right now. But you heard Christopher tonight. I think Larry's a good guy in a difficult position. Are you really afraid he's involved in this?"

"I can't say for sure. But we don't know him well."

"Christopher's known him longer than we have. And you and I have both worked with him — me in the orchard, you on the house. What's your read on him?"

"He doesn't open up easily."

"Seth, that's evasive. Do you trust him? Do you think he's honest? Or is he a drug lord in the making?"

"I'd go with the first two, but I'm not one hundred percent sure where his loyalties lie."

Seth's lack of commitment was annoying Meg. "Well, I for one choose to believe in him. That's what my gut says. I don't want to go through life mistrusting every new person I meet, wondering if they're sincere or if they're hiding something. I may be wrong some of the time, but I'd rather believe the best of people than the worst."

"Meg . . ." Seth seemed to be at a loss for words. "I can't tell you what to do or what not to do, and I won't even try. But please, be careful? Having faith in people is a good thing, but if you guess wrong . . . I don't want to lose you."

"I know. Maybe I'm just clinging to what I thought Granford was, and what living here with you would be like, but all that kind of fell apart over the past week. I'm happy with you, Seth, but I don't want to live in a bubble. I want to fix this, as far as it can be fixed. But I'm not some starry-eyed crusader either. Look, tomorrow you can talk to Art again, and I'll talk to Larry, and then we'll see where we are. Okay? Maybe the drug unit is doing it right and they'll have it all wrapped up before breakfast."

"We can hope. Upstairs?"

"Yes, before I fall over."

Meg slept the sleep of the just, whatever the heck that was, or more likely she was exhausted by the events of the day and by the stress of their current situation. It was Saturday, right? Not that it made much difference in her current situation. Seth had promised to talk with Art yet again, and she was going to talk with Larry, armed with what she knew now. The bottom line was, she trusted Larry. He was unpolished and inexperienced in some ways, but he was a hard worker. Sure, peddling drugs would be easy money for him, but he seemed to be committed to farming and wasn't looking for easy profits. And even if she was wrong about him, she firmly believed he wouldn't hurt her, or betray her to the other guys at the house. He couldn't have had anything to do with the shot that shattered her car window. Could he?

Larry came by about ten, looking for Seth. Seth told him, "I've got some paperwork to finish up, but why don't you wait here? I won't be long."

"Yeah, okay," Larry said, looking at his feet.

"You want some coffee, Larry?" Meg said, hating the chirpy tone in her voice. She sounded like some sitcom housewife from the fifties. But she had to admit to herself that she was nervous. "Sit down."

Larry sat and waited silently for the coffee she had promised. When she'd slid a filled mug in front of him, she sat in the chair opposite. "Larry, we have to talk."

"You're firing me," he said flatly.

"No! Nothing like that. You're doing a great job, and you know far more than I do about apples and orchards. This is about something else."

"What?" he asked, then waited expectantly.

Meg took a deep breath. "Larry, you've been living in Seth's house for a couple of months now, right?

"About that. Why?"

"Because there have been things happening this past week that really upset me, and Seth too. Jenn's death. The bullet through my car window. They could be accidental, but I don't really believe that. You've told me a bit about the guys you're living with, but maybe there are some things you haven't said? I know you don't like to make waves, but this may be important." Meg stopped herself from going overboard and saying it was a matter of life and death — even though it actually was. "What can you tell me?"

Larry looked down at his hands, clenched together on the table. Meg guessed he was wrestling with how to answer her, and she didn't interrupt. Finally he said, "I knew Jenn. Better than I told you."

"Oh?" That wasn't what Meg had expected to hear.

"Look, I never knew many girls before I left the farm. I was always busy working. And I was a hick with crummy clothes and a bad haircut, and I got kind of average grades in school, and I didn't play any sports, and I could never figure out what to say. So when Jenn started talking to me, a while back, I figured it was some kind of con. That she wanted something. Not that she was interested in me."

"So what happened?" Meg asked cautiously.

"She really came on to me, and I didn't know what to do. Then she told me she was new in town and didn't have anyplace to stay, and maybe she could crash at the house? I told her there weren't any empty rooms. And then she said, maybe she could stay with me? Like, in the same room?"

"What did you say?"

"What do you think? Yeah, she was a couple of years older than me, and I didn't get any real vibe that she was into me, but I wasn't about to say no."

"How long ago was this?"

"Three weeks ago, maybe. Something like that."

"So Jenn moved in with you and made it look like she was your girlfriend?"

"Hey, it's not like anybody talked about

that kind of stuff. And there were people in and out of the place all the time. One more didn't make that much difference. I don't know if anybody was paying attention."

"So things were good, up until the time she died?"

"Yeah, pretty much. She spent a lot of time talking with the other guys, but that was cool."

"So what happened when she was killed?" Meg was pretty sure that Larry hadn't shared this information with Art, about Jenn the pretend girlfriend. But Meg could see that it made sense from Jenn's perspective: she'd zeroed in on that particular group of guys as the linchpins of the drug traffic in Granford and nearby, and she had needed a way to get closer to them. Larry had provided the perfect patsy, but that also meant that Jenn had judged him to be harmless.

"One day she said she had things to do," Larry said. "She went out in the afternoon and didn't come back. And Seth found her."

"Where were the other guys those days?"

"They weren't around — you know, job, classes and stuff. I was over here helping Seth, or in my room with music on, so I don't know where people were. Meg, can I ask you something?" When she nodded, Larry said, "You working with the police?"

"Kind of. Unofficially. It's not the first time, not that I went looking to get involved with what they do, but some things have been kind of personal. And Art's a good friend. But the Northampton State Police Narcotics Unit is leading the investigation at the moment, not Homicide, and I'm not their favorite person. Larry, do you know what it means, that they're in charge?"

"That there are drugs involved. I wondered when you'd get around to that."

"Because you knew there was drug activity going on at the house?"

"I thought, maybe. But I didn't want to get involved, so I kind of ignored it."

Meg nodded. "Larry, Christopher told me about your background. I can understand why you didn't want to get involved. But did you know that Jenn was already mixed up in it?"

"Dealing?"

"No. She was writing a story for the Boston paper about the growth of drug traffic in this area. She must have gathered enough information to know that the other guys at the house were part of that, and she wanted to get inside. That's why she . . ."

"Came on to me," Larry said flatly. "I never did think she was hot for me, but that was okay. And then something went wrong, right?"

"So it seems. Larry, looking back, did you see anything like evidence of buying and selling drugs at the house?"

"A lot of people kept dropping by, but they didn't stay long. Some of them were pretty sketchy types, and some were pretty twitchy when they showed up. I'm not stupid — I figured something was up, but I didn't really know anything. I didn't want to, I guess. I wasn't part of it, but I figured the police might have other ideas. I didn't know if the police might come after Seth, since it's his place. So I just played stupid."

"Did anything change after Jenn was killed?"

"I told you, I wasn't really buddies with the other guys. They'd say something like, 'Tough luck, man' and leave it at that."

If what Larry said was true about their response, it suggested that Jenn hadn't blown her cover at the house — or the guys were good actors. "And you never saw any guns at the house?"

"No. Not that I was looking or anything. Plenty of places to hide things like that there."

"Seth and I have wondered why Jenn's body was left so close to the house, and this house too. Wouldn't it have made more sense to leave her somewhere that she wouldn't be found, or not quickly?"

Larry shrugged. "Maybe. Unless they thought it would look like she got shot by a sloppy hunter who was afraid to come forward."

"That was certainly everyone's first thought, but the evidence didn't support it. Do you know much about hunting?"

"Not really. My dad used to bag a deer now and then, and we'd freeze the meat. He didn't pay much attention to the rules, or things like licenses."

"So you don't know that this isn't the regular hunting season now, at least in this state."

"Why would I? I don't hunt. I don't have a gun."

Meg nodded again. "What we think is that Jenn was probably shot a couple of hours before she was found, and then someone took her out to that patch of woods and fired off another shot to make anyone who might be listening think that was when she was killed. So whoever did it didn't have a very high opinion of our local police — they probably thought they'd just see it as an accident, end of story. But that story didn't hold together, for a number of reasons. Do

271

you know where the other guys were that afternoon?"

"We talked about that before. They were always in and out. I didn't keep track."

"Nothing unusual that day? Did Jenn go out?"

"Yeah, right after lunch, I think. I saw her car leave. Hey, anybody found it yet?"

"Not that I've heard," Meg said. And Jenn had never come back. But nobody had known she was dead — except her killer.

There was one more thing Meg wanted to explore with Larry. "Larry, you told me a couple of days ago that you recognized the guy who came to my door asking about Jenn. Right?"

"Yeah, I saw him up at the house. Never talked to him, though."

"Was this before or after Jenn disappeared?"

"I'm not really sure — I wasn't keeping track. I know he was around after, but he was like a lot of the other guys — stopped by for a while, then left. He wasn't exactly hanging around talking."

"But it was more than once. A few times?"

"Yeah, I guess. Why?"

Well, in for a penny, in for a pound, Meg thought. "Larry, it turns out that the guy — his name is Justin — is actually a reporter for the same paper as Jenn was. We think he wanted a piece of her story." *Or more?* "Jenn was more senior, better known than he was, and he was hungry to get ahead. But that doesn't mean we can prove he had anything to do with her death. Maybe he was just following the same trail as she was. And I don't want to accuse him of murder just because he wanted a big story."

"Yeah, I get that," Larry said. After a long pause, he added, "What if he was involved?"

"In what? Selling drugs?"

Larry shrugged. "He was hanging around. So maybe he was selling to the other guys. Or supplying."

Damn, she hadn't thought of that. Now she'd have to.

"That's a good point. Larry, will you talk with Art? Tell him the whole story? He's a good guy, and he's on our side, but the state police keep shutting him out because he's just a local cop. I'm not looking to embarrass them, but I'd really like to find out what happened and lay this problem to rest. Are you willing?"

After a long pause, Larry finally said, "Yeah. I will. You've been good to me, given me a chance. Besides, it's the right thing to do."

"Thank you."

23

When Seth returned, Art was with him. Seth explained quickly, "Sorry, Meg, Larry — I gave Art a call when I reached my office, and we decided we should deal with our problem sooner rather than later. Larry, Meg told you what we were thinking?"

Larry ducked his head. "Yeah. I'm sorry I didn't tell you all everything, but I didn't think I had much to tell. I guess I was just trying to keep out of the whole mess, but that didn't exactly work, did it?"

"Larry," Art began, "Seth told me a bit about your family history, and I can understand why you didn't want to open that can of worms. Maybe you're right, that the state police would jump to conclusions and take the easy way out, but I'm not like that — which may be why they don't like me much. I would be grateful if you'd fill me in on what you know, and I promise I won't take it any further unless it's relevant to solving

Jenn's murder. Which, by the way, is my primary interest here, even though I'm not part of the investigation, since it's reasonable to guess that she died in my town. I have no desire to mess with the drug trade around here and will be happy to leave that to the guys from Northampton. If that's even possible, that is, because Jenn's death is tied into it somewhere. Anyway, let's just sit down and pool our information and see where it leads us, and we can sort out who should hear it when we're done. Fair enough?"

"Yeah," Larry said. "Everybody says you're a fair guy. And I know the guys at the house didn't much like you — they were always worried that you'd bust them for making too much noise, or exceeding the parking limits, or maybe something else made-up, just to annoy them."

"I don't work that way, Larry. You know, one thing nobody's talked about is where these three guys came from, before they moved here. Well, first, did they know each other before they moved in together?"

Larry shrugged. "I didn't get tight with them. They seem to get along fine, but I don't know if they moved here in a pack or just happened to end up together."

Seth held up a hand. "I'm partly to blame.

I'm new to this landlord stuff and I didn't think it through, so I never asked for an application or a credit check or references. Of course, they could have lied about just about anything, but they must have been really happy when I more or less said I didn't care about those details."

"Well, you sure made things easy for them, but I guess I'll forgive you. For now," Art said. "Actually, what I was asking was where the guys came from. Another state? A Massachusetts city? Canada?"

Meg, Seth and Larry looked blank. "Well, if it was Canada, it wasn't the French part," Larry finally volunteered. "No accents."

"Art," Meg began, "we've talked before about why it looks like whoever killed Jenn knew something about weapons but not about hunting regulations or living in a rural area. You still think that's correct?"

"Could be. Might point to someone who's lived in a city but was part of a group that used guns. Of course, this is only guesswork."

"Where are most of the drugs coming from these days?" Seth asked.

"I've read the memos, so to speak," Art told him. "Mostly north of here, I think. Depends on local regulations, and how hard the police in other places are looking."

"So nothing conclusive?" Seth said.

"Nope. For the two guys who claim to be in school, has anybody checked if they're actually enrolled and taking classes?"

"That's a bit beyond us, Art," Meg told him. "But I bet Christopher could find out."

Art sighed. "Okay, how much do Lydia and Christopher know about this whole mess?"

"About as much as we do," Seth said.

"Well, I guess it's safe to say that they aren't vigilantes and won't take matters into their own hands," Art muttered.

"I truly doubt that," Seth said, suppressing a smile. "But as I just told you, they did point out the increase in the frequency of visitors who stay for only a short while. That road at the top of the hill is usually pretty quiet, so they noticed the change."

"Yeah, yeah, I get it — it certainly looks like quick drug buys. But that's not conclusive. And it does not explain why anyone at the house would kill Jenn. Even if she knew what the guys were doing, she was looking for a story, and she was in the ideal position to get one, up close and personal, if she was spending any kind of time at the house."

Meg interrupted. "Art, I think you need to hear what Larry was telling me before you arrived. Larry? About the guys at the house, but particularly about Justin."

Art looked startled. "Justin? The guy who came here looking for Jenn?"

"Yes," Meg said. "Did Seth fill you in on what we learned in Boston?"

"That this Justin guy was a colleague of Jenn's at the paper?" Art said. "Yeah, he did. And we know he lied to me, and then he lied to you. Or at least gave a made-up story. Fooled me. I should have been wondering why he thought Granford was a likely place to look for her."

"Do you remember *when* he lied to you?" Meg demanded.

"Uh . . . after we knew that Jenn was dead?" Art guessed.

"Convenient, don't you think?" Meg added. "Larry, tell him what you know."

"This Justin was kind of a regular at the house. Seth's house, I mean."

Art suddenly looked more alert. "Before or after Jenn was dead?"

"After, or at least that's when I saw him. But maybe once or twice before. Jenn came and went a lot. But she was staying with me. In my room, I mean."

"Something romantic going on?" Art asked.

Larry shrugged. "Not really. She had her own car, and I'm pretty sure Justin didn't

278

show up when she was in the house — maybe he was watching to make sure she was out of the way. But he seemed pretty tight with the other guys, after."

"Let me get this straight," Art said. "Jenn found herself a way to stay in the house — by bunking with you, I mean — that she probably guessed was a hotspot for drug selling. Did she talk to you about that at all?"

"No. Maybe she figured I was too dumb to figure it out myself, or I knew what was going on but didn't care. We never talked about it. But she hung out with the guys a lot, when they were around."

"And Justin knew her from Boston but you can't say whether they crossed paths?"

"Yeah, that's right," Larry said, then shut up.

Art leaned back in his chair. "Okay, so we have one *Boston Globe* reporter who has somehow wormed her way into a drug house and convinced everybody that she was an out-of-work waitress just hanging out in this part of the world. And then we've got this Justin, also a *Boston Globe* reporter, who just happens to end up at the same place at the same time as Jenn but stays out of sight as long as she was alive. You think they were working together? Trying to get two angles on what was going on?"

Meg shook her head. "I doubt it. Toby, the friend of my Boston friend, is *also* a *Boston Globe* reporter, and he said that Justin was all about Justin. He wanted to make a name for himself, and teaming up with Jenn, while it looks like a good idea in theory, would not have been his style. He'd want to claim all the credit."

"And you got all this from one conversation over lunch at a busy restaurant, from someone who didn't know either of them well?"

"Well, yes," Meg admitted. "But I gather the bullpen, or whatever they call it at the paper, was kind of like a fishbowl, and everybody heard bits and pieces of information and could put them together. I think Toby — and probably a number of other people — knew that Jenn was working on something she thought could be big, although they might not have known what. And then she was gone for a couple of weeks. And Justin, who was pushy and acted like he was entitled, wanted a piece of it, and maybe he was smart enough to figure out what she was up to, but we doubt that Jenn wanted to share."

"And then Jenn died," Art said flatly. "How convenient for everybody. No big story to mess up their drug operation."

"Yes," Meg said. "Shot by an unknown someone who might know something about weapons, if that hole in my window is any indication, but who doesn't know much about hunting and state regulations."

"It's pretty thin, Meg. An awful lot of 'maybes.' "

"I know. But Justin lied. Not that that proves anything in itself, but if he had to lie about why he was here and wanted to talk to me, it makes me think there's something fishy going on."

Art considered that for a moment, then said, "You sure it's not because you want to believe that journalists are honest? Maybe he didn't want to blow his cover, and thought he still had a shot at Jenn's story? Now that she's dead, the headlines might be juicier, and his name could be in bigger print. If he ever writes the damn thing. Larry, did Jenn take any notes?"

Larry shook his head. "Nobody had much stuff there at the house, and nobody locked doors, so it wouldn't have been safe for her to leave notes or something around the house, in case anybody was looking. Nobody locked cars either, so she wouldn't have left anything there."

"Did she have a computer?"

"No."

"Carrying a computer around might have blown her cover, Art," Meg said.

"Maybe she wrote letters? You know, the kind on paper? And mailed them to her editor, or even to herself at the paper?" Art was looking increasingly frustrated. "If the editor has them, then the narcotics unit should know about it. They haven't said a word, to me or Marcus, but that's the way they've been operating from the beginning. So maybe the notes exist, but we're not likely to find out what they say."

"Where's Marcus in all this?" Seth said suddenly.

"Got me. He hasn't called or written. I feel sooo alone," Art said sarcastically. "And here I've given him every juicy tidbit we've found."

"So where does that leave us?" Meg demanded. "We have a nice theory, even if there are a few holes in it. Where's Justin at the moment? Is he staying somewhere around here? You know, he could simply commute from Boston — it's only a couple of hours, and he could look like he was doing business as usual as long as he shows his face at the paper now and then."

"When was the last time anyone around here saw him?" Art asked. "Larry, has he been around the house lately?"

Larry shook his head. "I've been spending most of my spare time here working on the tiny house, so I probably wouldn't have seen him."

"But Toby said that Justin hadn't been around the paper much either — we met at a restaurant, not there, just in case Justin saw Seth and me and thought something was going on."

Art sighed again. "Meg, Seth, there's really not much to act on here."

"Art," Seth said, "I own that house. I should have a right to inspect the place as needed."

"Any structural problems? Plumbing? Electric? Giant rats running around?"

"You mean, if I need an excuse? Hard to sabotage plumbing from a distance, but I bet I could jigger with the wiring connections and hope they call me to find out what the problem is. I'd rather not go with the rats."

"Okay," Art began. "Say you make the lights go on and off or whatever, and you get inside the house. What would you be looking for?"

"Uh . . . I don't know? Jenn's notes? A small recorder that she hid somewhere?"

"That we aren't even sure exists," Art

pointed out. "Next idea?"

"Bloodstains? Or bloody clothing? A recently fired weapon?"

"Seems unlikely anyone would shoot her with a rifle inside the house, and that's what the evidence shows. More likely somebody would have arranged to meet her where they couldn't be seen, like your woods, Meg, or even farther away. Anyway, physical evidence would be easy to get rid of — just burn the clothes. Assuming her killer got blood on himself trying to move her. As for whatever information she collected, he could pitch the recorder into the swamp — no one will ever find it. Next?"

"The murder weapon?" Seth suggested. "Wouldn't take much to hide it. But they don't know the house well, or all the hidey-holes. I can't guess whether they thought anyone would ever search for anything there. That electrical excuse would come in handy for searching, because you've got to get behind walls and under floorboards to follow the wiring."

"Maybe. The murder weapon wouldn't belong to your family, right, Seth?"

"Nope. Dad was a plumber and he had no interest in hunting. Neither did Mom."

"You and your brother never found an old rifle up in the attic and took it out to take potshots at trees?"

"No. There was an old shotgun, in the attic, I think, but we were too scared to try it, if it even worked. But maybe one of the guys brought his own rifle and stashed it somewhere."

"And likely got rid of it as soon as Jenn was found dead." Art stood up and stretched, then paced around the kitchen. "Guys, I hate to rain on your parade, but I don't see anything I can do. Under normal circumstances — whatever those are these days — I could probably search the house, make up some story about you seeing figures skulking around after dark, and I'd have your permission, Seth, of course. But with the eyes of the drug unit watching everything we do, that's not going to work, and we'll have made some enemies if we tried."

"So you're giving up, Art?" Meg demanded.

"What else can I do? We have a dead woman, shot with a twenty-two rifle and dumped in your woods. We have a sketchy guy who seems to be pretending to be someone he isn't, who claimed he was looking for her. We have three guys living in the house up the hill who may be drug dealers, or scouts for some bigger drug group, or they may be your typical messy, lazy twenty-somethings just hanging out. There may be more street traffic up there than before, but it could be that the guys just like to party. And on top of all that, I have no jurisdiction here, and Marcus got told to back off. Whatever information exists has to be in the hands of the drug unit, and they aren't sharing. Have I missed anything?"

Larry spoke up suddenly, almost reluctantly. "I haven't told you everything. Jenn did give me something to keep for her. She said she didn't want to leave it at the house, and would I take it and hide it somewhere. And not ask any questions. So I did. Hide it, I mean."

"Why the bloody hell didn't you come forward with this sooner?" Art all but yelled.

"Because I didn't know who to trust. Because I wasn't sure how she died or who killed her. Because I was afraid you cops would think I had something to do with it. You want more reasons?"

Art took a deep breath. "Sorry. No, I get it. So is it still safe?" When Larry nodded, Art asked, "Will you let me see it? If it's something personal, whatever's on it doesn't have to leave this room."

Larry glanced at Meg, who gave him a small nod. "Yeah, sure. It's in a container that I put next to the foundation of the house Seth and I are working on — I didn't think anybody would go poking around there. Don't worry, it's sealed up tight. I never expected that it would stay there long."

"Then let's go collect it and see what Jenn left for us."

24

Hearing Larry's announcement, Meg was torn between frustration and elation. How could he have not known it could be important? Jenn certainly had thought so. But the flip side was, Larry had little reason to trust anyone in his life. He'd made a promise to Jenn and he'd kept it, so clearly it was important to him, and he'd kept the information safe. She was touched that she — *they* — had won Larry's trust, but she was also itching to find out what Jenn had left behind.

"When did she give you this?" Meg asked.

"Not long before she . . . died. She didn't make a big deal about it, just said, 'Put this somewhere safe, will you?' So I did. But if I think about it now, maybe she was worried about something."

Or someone? Meg asked herself.

"And you didn't ask what it was or why it had to be hidden?" Art asked.

"No. It wasn't any of my business. But I don't think she trusted the guys at the house."

"Art, maybe she'd seen Justin prowling around town," Meg said, "and that made her nervous. Maybe she didn't trust him either. And she didn't have a computer with her, so she couldn't exactly email whatever she'd collected. I've never checked — are there computers for public use at the library?"

"Sure," Art told her, "but somebody might have thought it was out of character for her to be on the computer there. She was trying to be careful, and obviously she had a good reason to be, given what happened."

"Maybe we should find out what it is?" Seth suggested. "If she didn't have a computer, it must be a voice recording. Or handwritten notes, or some combination of those."

"Guys, why don't we just go get it and find out what she gave Larry?" Art said, his voice impatient.

"What, you don't want to call the state narcotics people and wait for them to carry it off to their secret cavern and decipher it?" Seth shot back in much the same tone.

"Seth, let's just get this done." Now Art sounded testy. "Can you show us where you put it, Larry?"

"Yeah, sure. We'd just finished repointing the old foundation, but we hadn't started on the framing. So I kind of hid it next to one of the old piers from the chicken house — I figured I could go back and get it if Jenn needed it. Don't worry, I sealed it up real well, but I didn't look at any of it. She asked me not to."

"Let's go, then," Art said briskly.

They all grabbed coats and trooped out the back door, crossing the yard to the growing small structure at the rear of the property. "You guys have gotten a lot done since the last time I saw it," Art commented.

"It's small, and the work goes fast. Want one?" Seth told him.

"I'd like a little more room. But it might make a good man-cave, as long as you heat it."

"Of course we're heating it. All the comforts of home, just smaller."

When they reached the building, Larry went around to the side and started scrabbling at the base of the foundation, where it met the dirt. Then Meg looked up to see Justin approaching. "Oh, sh . . . oot. Art, we've got company. Wonder what story he'll give us this time?" Out of the corner of her eye Meg saw Larry slip something into an inside pocket of his jacket and zip the pocket shut.

When Justin was close enough to make himself heard he called out, "Hey, I'm glad I found all of you together. I need to talk with you."

"Find your girlfriend?" Art asked neutrally.

"Well, that's one thing I want to talk about. Can we go inside? I'm freezing."

"Follow me," Seth told him, and led the way. Art and Meg fell back, trailed by Larry.

"How do we play this, Art?" Meg asked in a low voice.

"Pretend we don't know anything. Let him talk. Then we'll see. Would he recognize you, Larry?"

"Maybe, but I doubt it. I mostly stayed out of everybody's way."

And if Justin was busy playing drug dealer or buyer or whatever, he would have dismissed Larry as unimportant and concentrated on the other guys, Meg thought.

They all crowded into the kitchen and shuffled awkwardly. "There's more room in the dining room, if you all want to sit down. Anyone want coffee?"

"Please," Justin said, still rubbing his hands together to warm them.

Meg set about once again making coffee,

while the men milled around the dining room table trying to establish some sort of social hierarchy. Seth was the master of the house — give him points for that. Art was an official representing the law, but he didn't want to push that role until he saw what Justin might have to say, so he was probably going to play the bumbling country cop to start. Larry was kind of the invisible man, who kept his head down and his mouth shut. Justin was the guest of honor, who had requested this gathering and who presumably had something he wanted to say. And she was the Eternal Coffee Maker. At least nobody had asked her to be a good girl and take notes — yet.

She put together a tray with the coffeepot, cups, spoons, sugar and cream. She debated briefly about adding a plate of cookies, but this didn't seem like a cookies occasion, not if it resulted in identifying Jenn's murderer. She carried the tray in and set it in the middle of the table, then took a chair next to Seth. He took the lead. "What was it you wanted to talk about, Justin?"

"I've been an idiot, I'll admit that up front," Justin began. "I've made a fool of myself, and pretended I could fool other people, and I may have contributed to getting Jenn killed."

"Let's start at the beginning, Justin," Meg said. "We all know that Jenn was a journalist working for the *Boston Globe* — she told the state police that when she first arrived. She said that she was doing research for a big article about the growth of the drug trade in this area, which seems to have become a hot new market over the past couple of years. She chose to go undercover and wormed her way into the house up the hill there, and used Larry here as her cover story. The house belongs to Seth, my husband, and Larry works for me in my orchard. We believe she thought that one or more of the other guys sharing the house were involved with selling drugs and she wanted to see how it worked from the inside. Are we right in guessing that she didn't share her plans with anyone at the newspaper, including you? She might have told her boss, we thought, but it wouldn't have been common knowledge there. How'm I doing?"

"Better than I did, at the beginning," Justin admitted. "Look, I really admired Jenn. She was smart, and really good at the job. I wanted to be like her in a couple of years. But she was pretty much a lone operator and she didn't need a sidekick to slow her down. I picked up a few bits and pieces of information in the newsroom, enough to get a hint about what she was doing, and one day I simply followed here out here. That part wasn't hard. She didn't see me, or at least not at first. I hung around for a few days, trying to stay out of sight. I didn't know enough then to stick my nose in, so I just watched, and paid attention to who was doing what. And then she was dead."

Art finally spoke. "Did you have anything to do with her death? Did you see anything, overhear a comment that maybe she was getting too close and couldn't be trusted?"

Justin shook his head vehemently. "Nothing like that — mostly I wasn't close enough to see or hear anything. I didn't want to mess up her game plan. And I didn't know what was going on inside the house, just that a lot of people were dropping by and leaving quickly."

"Do you know this area?" Art asked.

Justin shook his head "Not really. I didn't grow up around here. I'm really more of a city boy, although I went to some good schools. So I'd never seen this part of the state until Jenn came out here."

"So just to be clear," Art went on, "you did not see anyone threaten or harm Jenn, or drag her out into the woods and kill her?"

"Of course not!" Justin protested. "I would have told someone! You, or that homicide officer in Northampton. Somebody!"

"All right. So Seth found her body in the woods, or rather, his dog Max did." At the sound of his name Max raised his head briefly, then went back to sleep in his warm corner of the floor. "And Seth called me, and I called the state police, who handle homicides around here."

"But why did the news say the body of an unidentified woman was found?" Justin asked. "And never reported who she was? Somebody must have known," Justin said.

Art studied Justin. "The guys in Northampton knew. I talked to the homicide detective there, and it turned out that the narcotics unit told him to keep his mouth shut because they were closing in on busting a nest of drug dealers and they didn't want to spook them. They wanted to make a big splash and get all the glory — and, to be fair, probably to send a message to any other dealers who were thinking of moving in around here. Let us say that Homicide Detective Marcus was not happy about that, but he went along with the program because he had to — orders from the top. But I believe he was unaware of where Jenn had been since she arrived, and who she was associating with."

"And then I showed up and almost made a mess of the whole thing," Justin said glumly. "I talked to him — that was all right, wasn't it? And he told me he didn't know anything about my nonexistent missing girlfriend."

"Sure. None of us knew much at that point, and you were looking for your so-called girlfriend because you were worried about her. All perfectly reasonable. Maybe even logical, given that this is a small town and everybody seems to know everybody else. But nobody knew anything about the woman you described, and we weren't supposed to call attention to the body that was found, although I'm going to guess that a few people around here might have put two and two together, but they didn't tell me about their suspicions. And your story really was kind of weak."

"Huh," Justin said, as if surprised by Art's comment. "But you bought into it anyway?"

"I didn't exactly doubt it, at the time," Art told him.

Justin turned to Meg. "And then I came and tried out the same story on you, Meg."

"Yes, but I knew it wasn't true. Art and I are friends, and since Jenn was found on my land, he shared some of the details with me. He knew I wouldn't spread it around."

"But you knew enough to know I was a phony."

"Yes. Tell me this, Justin: What were you looking for? What did you plan to do?"

"I guess I figured that if the dead woman was in fact Jenn, then maybe I could pick up where she had left off. I mean, if somebody killed her, she must have found something, and I thought maybe I could figure it out."

"So you never bought into the hunting accident story?" Art asked. When Justin shook his head, Art went on, "Do you know anything about weapons? Hunting?"

"Hell, no! I grew up in Connecticut. I've never fired a gun in my life. Of course, if I wanted to avoid suspicion, I'd say that anyway, wouldn't I?"

Art didn't respond to that comment. "And you don't know anything about state regulations regarding hunting in Massachusetts?"

"No, I do not."

Art turned to Meg. "What do you think?"

Meg looked levelly at Justin. "Based on what we knew — and saw — we were guessing that whoever shot Jenn knew something about weapons but didn't know much about the legal details of hunting around here. It could have been written off as a hunting accident, if there hadn't been so many odd things attached already. But that was the story that got fed to the public. There are probably some people who are still hoping the shooter will turn himself in. Although fatal hunting accidents, I'm told, are pretty rare in this state and in most other places. Whoever shot Jenn didn't think it through, and he made mistakes."

"But who killed her?" Justin demanded.

"We still don't know," Art said. "We do know she wasn't shot where she was found, but we don't know how far she was carried before she was dumped. We aren't sure why she was dumped on Meg's property, since Meg had nothing to do with any of this. Or maybe that was why — Meg isn't a hunter, she didn't know the woman, and she had no reason to kill her."

Justin leaned forward on his elbows. "But under the circumstances, the obvious candidates are those guys up the hill. The fact that Jenn planted herself there suggests that she suspected they were dealers and wanted evidence to confirm it. And some colorful details to enhance her story — you know, the human interest angle."

It made Meg sad that Justin seemed to care more about the story than about a woman he had known and worked with. "Justin, how old are you?" she asked suddenly.

"Twenty-five. I've been with the paper since college."

"And how much do you know about drugs?"

Justin looked wary, his eyes shifting between Art and the others at the table. Finally he sighed. "Not a heck of a lot. I mean, I know the names and the facts, but I've never, uh, experimented. Maybe a little weed in college. But not the hard stuff — the big-money stuff."

"Why on earth did you think you were the right person to write this story?" Seth demanded. "You were stumbling around blind."

Justin straightened his back and looked squarely at Seth. "You're right. I was hungry for a big story to jump-start my career at the paper, and I knew Jenn was on to something. She was a smart woman and a good writer, and I truly admired her. If by bumbling around in Granford I set off something that led to her death, I am truly sorry. Chief, do the state drug guys have a case yet? Why haven't they moved on the dealers yet? And the murder?"

"I wish I could tell you, Justin. Maybe

they're still waiting for all the details, or to catch someone important in the act. Maybe they know who's involved but they have no evidence that would hold up in court and they'd lose their chance, and all the players would scatter to another small town or towns and start over. It's not all that hard to do. Or maybe they figure that shutting down the drug trade and saving a lot of lives is more important than catching whoever killed one nosy reporter."

"So what is anybody going to do about it?" Justin demanded.

"We're hoping Jenn left us a trail of breadcrumbs to follow, and maybe something like evidence. She entrusted what she had to Larry here, since it seems she didn't think she could hide it at the house. We haven't looked at it yet."

"Can we?" Justin looked like an eager kid. "I mean, I'm sure you need to give it to the state police, but can't we take a look at it first?"

"I don't see any good reason why we can't," Art told him. "I think we've earned it."

25

"So what've you got?" Justin demanded.

"Slow down, son," Art said. "This is not your party. Jenn gave this to Larry, so more likely it's his party, or Meg's, or maybe Seth's. Or even mine. You're at the back of the line, and if you try to shove your way into the middle of this, I'll boot you out. Got it?"

"Yes. Sorry." Justin seemed to shrink a little.

"Okay, so let's review. Jenn arrived in the area, what, a month ago? When did she first show up at the house? Larry, you remember?"

"Not right away. Three weeks ago, maybe?"

"Okay. So let's say she arrived in the area a month ago and spent some time scoping the place out before she made a move. Justin, did she ever show her face at the newsroom in that time?"

Justin shrugged. "Maybe. I wasn't watching, but it would surprise me if she stayed away as long as a month. She'd probably want to touch base with her editor."

Meg made a mental note to check with Toby about whether he'd seen Jenn in the right time frame.

"Okay," Art resumed, "so she's figured out the lay of the land and zeroed in on Seth's house and its occupants as the kind of setup she was looking for. She starts hanging out there, and she decides you aren't really part of the gang, Larry, so she figures you're safe and she makes a play for you and moves in. Right?"

Larry avoided his eyes. "More or less."

"And that would be between two and three weeks ago. Anybody else have a girl hanging around?"

Larry shook his head. "Nope. Well, some came and went, but nobody stayed."

"Got it. So Jenn had two weeks max to observe what went on and who was involved before she was killed. Justin, where were you?"

"I made a couple of quick trips out here from Boston, once I knew where to find her, but I didn't stay around — I didn't want to risk her seeing me."

"What did you think you were going to

do?" Seth asked. "Demand to share her byline? Blackmail her? Did you have a plan?"

"I don't know," Justin said, sounding like a sulky child. "I wanted to see how things played out. Or maybe I was thinking I'd sweep in and rescue her from the big bad drug dealers, if things went sour."

"And claim a piece of the story," Seth added.

Justin didn't bother to answer that.

Art turned to Larry again. "Okay, Larry, you lived with these guys for a couple of months. I know you said you made a point of not hanging out with them, but you must have formed some kind of impression of them, singly or together. What were they like? Describe them for me."

Larry looked startled for a moment, then he started thinking. "Two of 'em — Mike Wilson and Tom Reilly — went to UMass, took classes. I'm not a hundred percent sure they were full-time students, but they were over there at least part of the time. Or at least out of the house at regular times. The third one, Ed Lopes, had a job. Not an office job, but he worked for some local factory or contractor. His hours were kind of all over the place — sometimes he was back in the afternoon, other times I didn't see him until the next day. It's not like we were keeping track of each other. We didn't cook together or anything. Me, I was usually down the hill here, with Meg or Seth."

"So there was no regular schedule — everybody was in and out and went their separate ways. You said there were parties, how often? Every night? Only Saturday night?"

"Somewhere between. And maybe parties makes them sound bigger than they were. Somebody, or a couple of people, would stop by, maybe grab a beer, hang out for a while, then leave again. Nobody stayed really long."

"And you never saw money change hands, or anybody hand over a bottle or a packet of pills?"

"No. But I never thought about it. Anyway, I was kind of busy with Jenn, so I wasn't paying attention."

"And what was she doing? Staying at the house or coming and going?"

"In more than out, I guess. Look, she made up a cover story, right? Like she got out of Boston because she needed a break, but she kind of hinted that there was a guy she'd rather not see again, so nobody should talk about her to anyone outside the house. To outsiders, I mean. Nobody else was supposed to know she was there."

"So that gave her an excuse to stay at the house and watch what was going on," Art said, almost to himself. "And somewhere in there she found time to put together some kind of notes, which she told you to hide. I guess we — and by that I mean me, a duly elected officer of the law — should examine whatever she left. You have any latex gloves, Meg?"

"What? Oh, maybe — I use them for cleaning sometimes, and for chopping garlic. You want to preserve any fingerprints there might be?"

"That's what I was thinking. Meg, you go get those gloves. Larry, hand over the goods." Art held out his hand.

Larry hesitated a moment, then reached into his pocket and pulled out a small box, about the size of a tin of Altoids, and dropped it into Art's palm. In the kitchen Meg rummaged around under the sink and returned with a pair of gloves, which she held out to Art without speaking.

"Should we be recording this?" she asked.

"Why? We aren't sure what we're going to find, or what we're going to do with it. If it's her market list we trash it. If it points the finger at someone, we're going to have to think about it." Art donned the gloves

305

and carefully peeled back the plastic that Larry had wrapped around the package. And the next layer and the next. "Good job keeping it dry, kid," he said. Meg wasn't sure if he was joking or not.

Nobody said a word as Art carefully extricated a neatly folded wad of paper, opened the small pile, and laid one sheet at a time on the table. Clearly the sheets all came from a single small notebook; the sheets measured maybe four by six inches, and many were covered with very small lettering in pencil. A couple of pages had columns of numbers and letters.

"Looks like license plate numbers," Art said. "Buyers, you think? Mostly in-state, but a few from farther away. Easy enough to run the plates, see who's who."

"What about the rest?" Meg asked.

"Names, for one thing. Short bios of the guys who were living there — not research, exactly, but things they said, places they mentioned, that kind of thing. Then we have which people came most often, which could be the suppliers. Mostly she got first names only — they must have been careful, or she couldn't get close enough to get more. Again, easy to run the names in our computer, see if they've got prior drug experience. Or any other kind."

"Like murder," Larry said, with a hint of bitterness.

"And that's all?" Justin said, incredulous.

Art turned on him. "What, you expected five thousand words of elegant prose? She was undercover, collecting information. She may have left us details of sellers and buyers. Frequency. Amounts bought. Money that came in. Hard to say, until we look through these pages with a magnifier. But the rest she kept in her head, for the story she was going to write. And now she never will."

"What are you going to do with it, Art?" Meg asked quietly.

"You mean, who do I give it to? I think I'd give it to Marcus. I can use some points with him, and he can show up the drug guys by handing them information they can use. Win-win, sort of. We all come out looking good."

"But who killed Jenn?" Larry asked.

"I doubt that's included in what she wrote. I think we need to look more carefully at what little she wrote about the people in the house. Not to see who appears to be the best candidate for killer, but because he has the most to lose. Could be money, could be reputation, could be his standing in the dealers' community, if there is such a thing. Or maybe he figured out what Jenn was up to and panicked."

"And just happened to have a twenty-two rifle with him?" Seth scoffed. "How did he lure Jenn out of the house to wherever she was killed, so he could do the deed? And why did he bring her back here and dump her?"

"A message to his colleagues? Or to the people he does business with? You know, 'Mess with me and this could happen to you.' He didn't have to know she was a journalist, just that she was a problem — too nosy. Maybe he thought she was working for the police. Maybe he and his pals were afraid she wanted a piece of the action. We may never know what he was thinking, and what gave her away."

"So leaving her to be found out back was intended as a warning. It was deliberate," Seth said.

"That'd be my guess. The problem was, he misjudged how hunting works around here and assumed nobody would look too closely. He probably didn't know that the state police were already on the trail."

"You want to call Marcus, tell him to come here because we have a present for him?" Seth asked.

Art sighed yet again. "That's probably the

best strategy. That way he doesn't have to put on a show for whoever's in his office, and it gives him a little time to think about how he wants to handle it. And it also makes it clear that we're all involved and we're watching."

Nobody around the table put up an argument, so Seth told Art, "Do it."

"Now?"

"Why not? Let's get it over with."

"You're right." Art stood up abruptly, fished his phone out of his pocket, and stalked toward the front parlor.

Meg's emotions were an unsettling mix of fear and excitement. This whole investigation might be over soon. But then again, it might not, since there were several groups of people involved and each group had its own agenda. She and her gang wanted this to be over. The drug unit wanted a big and highly public score, not just a roundup of a couple of amateurs. Marcus wanted to one-up the drug unit. Who was going to win?

"Anybody want to flip a coin to see whether he decides to show up or laughs in Art's face?" Seth asked.

"What's he got to lose?" Meg asked. "He doesn't have to say where he's going. Either he goes back to the office with a big win or he goes back and doesn't say anything."

"Is this a big win for around here?" Justin asked. "I mean, a house with a bunch of scruffy guys selling whatever stuff they've got? The real money's got to be someplace bigger, doesn't it? Holyoke? Springfield? Someplace like that?"

"Justin, I think you're missing the big picture here," Seth told him. "Until recently Granford was a sleepy little town where the same families had lived for a couple of centuries. Nobody had any reason to stop here. But it's close to some important college communities, particularly UMass, and it's invisibility turns out to be an asset. Nobody's looking for this kind of crime here, so it seems safe and it's easy to set up shop. What I think the dealers weren't counting on is that the residents here pay attention to what's going on, so if there's a flurry of unusual activity — like those cars coming and going at all hours — they notice, and they think about it. Like my mother. She's not on high alert for drug dealers, but she did comment that traffic has really picked up lately, only because the headlights shine into her bedroom windows. We're the ones who came up with a theory about why the traffic had increased, out here on a road that doesn't really go anywhere. The city guys wouldn't have thought about it."

"Hey, great image," Justin said, pulling a notebook out of his shirt pocket and scribbling a note on it. "So how did Jenn figure out what was going on?" he asked.

"I'd guess she did her homework," Seth said. "Like looking at maps. Pulling up local crime statistics. The presence of law enforcement — or lack of. All before she put together a plan and showed up to get involved on a more personal level. She used Larry to get into the house. You might want to follow her example, if you want a big story."

"It got her killed," Justin muttered.

"It did, and we may never know where things went wrong for her. But I'm going to guess that her story would have been better than anything you could write, because it would be 'real,' for want of a better word. The details would have been authentic, not pulled from the internet or a conversation in a bar. Face it, the world has gotten kind of scary when the boys next door in a quiet town turn out to be drug dealers."

Art returned to the dining room and said, "Marcus is on his way."

26

It took Detective William Marcus less than half an hour to arrive at Meg's door. Seth went to let him in. Marcus's first words were, "I hope to hell this isn't another wild-goose chase."

"Nice to see you too, Detective," Seth said. "Come on in. The gang's all here."

Marcus had never been a person to let his expression give much away, so he showed no surprise when he walked into the dining room and took in the group seated around the table. "Maybe you'd better introduce yourselves."

Art took the lead. "You know me, and Seth and Meg. The new faces are Larry Bennett, who's working for Meg in the orchard, and Justin Campbell, who's a junior reporter for the *Boston Globe.* He worked with Jenn Chambers. Why don't you sit down? This may take a while."

"Can I get you some coffee, Detective?"

Meg said, trying to keep a straight face while saying the tired line yet again.

"You got anything stronger?" he replied.

"Aren't you on duty?" Seth asked.

"Doesn't much matter. The only action around here seems to be this drug business and the murder, and I can't touch either one, even though the murder is part of my job, and the drug guys aren't listening to me. It's stupid, and it's a waste of time."

"Will Scotch do?" Meg asked.

"Sure." Marcus fell silent again. He really was in a foul mood, Meg noted, but she decided not to comment.

"Anybody else?" Meg scanned the faces around the table, then decided to bring the bottle and glasses and let people decide what they wanted to do. She was tired of playing waitress.

After a couple of minutes of glum silence, Marcus, Art and Seth helped themselves to a drink, followed by Meg. Marcus finally said. "Preston, you said you had information for me?"

"We do. And it was a joint effort, not just mine."

"Yeah, yeah, you all work and play together really nicely. What've you got?"

"A possible solution to Jenn Chambers's murder and how it's connected to the drug problem we have here in Granford."

Marcus swirled his Scotch in his glass. "Interesting — in one sentence you've told me you know who the dead girl was, you think she was murdered, and you're implying that she was looking at the drug dealers Seth has stashed in his house up there. Unless you want me to think she was a user. Tell me you've got more than a nice theory."

"We do," Art said calmly. "We have Jenn's notes. Not a lot of details, because she didn't have a computer or a cell phone with her, but enough to get you pointed in the right direction."

"Where've they been all along?"

"Jenn gave the notes to Larry here to keep safe — he was one of the guys sharing the house. He hid them away from the house, in case anybody went looking for them there. And in his — and our — defense, he didn't know what he had because everybody was sending such confusing signals or not telling the truth that he didn't realize what he had might be important. He was doing a favor for a friend, period. We only learned about them this morning."

"Why are you so sure this guy isn't just leading you on, sending you off in the wrong direction?" He stared coldly at Larry. Larry held his gaze.

"Because I've known him since last fall and worked with him," Meg said. "And so has Seth. We trust him, and so does Christopher Ramsdell. Why don't *you*?"

"He's not from around here, and his family history's a little murky."

"Has he ever been in trouble with the law?" Seth demanded.

"Not that I've found — yet."

"My father had a record, mostly small stuff," Larry finally spoke up. "You've probably already found that. Not me."

"Marcus, which side are you on?" Art said, clearly annoyed. "You want to hear what we've got, or do you have something more important to do?"

"Go ahead," he grumbled.

"And let us tell it in our own way."

"Just get on with it, will you?"

Art led off with the discovery of the body a week earlier, and the conclusions they'd drawn about the killing. He went on with the bits and pieces of information that had emerged since, from various sources — Lydia and Christopher, Larry, and most recently Justin — and how they'd fit them together. Marcus didn't comment, but he seemed to be listening. At the end of an hour, Art pulled out the papers that Jenn had left behind, now stored in a plastic sleeve that Meg had provided. "This was all she felt safe in recording, I think, or had time for. At least, we don't know of anything more, but we haven't gone through the house. That includes Larry's room. What we have seems to be a quick sketch of each of the guys living in the house, plus a list of what look like license plates, and a few other names, maybe guys who dropped by regularly — distributors or customers, it's not clear. The notes cover a period of a couple of weeks, up until just before Jenn died. That's when she gave them to Larry. She must have known that something had gone wrong."

"She trusted him?" Marcus glanced at Larry.

"So it seems. And he turned them over to us today."

"Where's this guy fit?" Marcus jerked his head at Justin.

Justin finally spoke. "I knew her before she ever got here. We worked at the same paper, but we weren't exactly friends. There were rumors at the paper that she was working on something big, and she wasn't around a lot. I started snooping and found she was coming out here, and then she stayed here for a while. I was hoping to get a piece of whatever she was working on, but we never had a chance to talk. After she died, your lot refused to ID the body publicly, which seemed odd to me, so I started nosing around, asking questions. That got me into the house up there, supposedly looking for her, but nobody was saying much."

"She know you were hanging around, following her?"

"I hope not — she wasn't supposed to. Maybe I wasn't as careful as I should have been. Or maybe I wasn't taking the whole thing seriously. I just wanted a story. I didn't think about the risks."

Marcus looked skeptical, but he didn't say anything. He hadn't yet touched the papers Art had laid on the table.

"What now?" Seth asked.

Marcus studied him for a moment. "You people have given me a nice tale, about some nasty drug dealers operating out of a rural house in Granford — your house, Seth Chapin. Part of this is based on a lot of traffic coming and going from that house, as reported by your mother. The dead woman was found on your wife's property. The dead woman was shacking up with your wife's employee before she was killed. What should I think?"

"You should think we're trying to help

you, Detective," Meg said. "We're just giving you the facts we've put together. We know you've been shut out of a homicide investigation on your own turf, and that doesn't make you very happy. We have no prior association with these people, except Larry, and we know nothing about drug dealing. All we want is to find who killed this woman and left her in my backyard. And while you're at it, could you arrest the drug dealers next door? Or won't the drug unit people let you?"

Marcus took a long swallow of his drink, apparently to stall for time. "Okay, say I believe you, and that you've actually put together some evidence. If I went by the book, I'd have to examine it and verify it, if I could do that without tipping anybody off. And then I'd have to plan an approach to the house and its current occupants. I'd have to have checked if they had criminal records or any history with other local police departments. I'm not trying to jerk you around, but this is just standard procedure. And of course you know that the circumstances aren't exactly normal. The narcotics unit is drawing up its own plans and they don't want me involved. They figure their drug bust trumps one dead journalist."

He drained his glass. "So my options are, trot back to Northampton and hand them what you've just given me and say, 'Pretty please, can we follow through on this?' Maybe, just maybe, they're ready to make their move and this would fit nicely. Or I hand this to them and they say, 'Didn't we tell you to stay out of this?' Or I take it to the police commissioner and explain the bind I'm in and maybe get permission to do something, which of course would tick off the narcotics unit. By the way, I'm not the commissioner's favorite person. Plus, she'd score more points with the public if she takes down a drug gang. So what odds would you give for my getting any support for going after your neighbors here?"

"Look," Art began, "we're not accusing you of dragging your feet or ignoring this. We know you're in a tough situation. But what would it take to override that? You want more bodies? Or a whole bunch of local kids who OD'd on whatever they're selling?"

"An immediate threat. A real and present danger, not a bunch of theories strung together that don't quite add up to probable cause. A signed invitation from a local drug lord? I really don't know."

Meg had been so focused on the discussion that she was startled when the phone rang. She answered it quickly and found it was Lydia.

"Meg, I don't want to worry you or Seth, but I heard what sounded like gunshots coming from Seth's house. At least, I think they were gunshots. I tried calling Art but he's not picking up."

"Because he's sitting in our kitchen, Lydia. I'll let him know. Have you heard any more since the first shots?"

"A couple, maybe. It's hard to tell — the windows are mostly closed, and I didn't want to go outside and check."

"I'll send Art over right now. You sit tight."

After she hung up, Meg hurried back to the dining room. "That was Lydia. She thinks she's heard gunshots coming from Seth's house."

Art stood up quickly. "So I'd better check it out ASAP."

"Want some company?" Marcus asked.

"Sure. If you're armed."

"I'm coming too," Seth said. "It's my house."

"So am I," Larry added. "I live there. I know who's who."

"Taking civilians along is not a good idea," Marcus cautioned.

"We're coming," Seth said. "Car or on foot?"

"Why don't you drive up and block the driveway?" Art suggested. "We'll go on foot — quieter that way. But I'd better tell my dispatcher what's up."

Two minutes later the motley crew took off up the hill. One homicide detective, one small-town police chief, and two civilians — one of whom was her husband, Meg thought, with a stab of fear. These drug people were not afraid of shooting at people, and she hoped that Marcus or Art would at least identify themselves as law enforcement before something awful happened. She shook herself and went back to the dining room, where Justin was still sitting at the table, starting glumly into space.

"You didn't want to go with the guys, Justin?" Meg asked. "It could make a good story." Now she wondered if *she* was being sarcastic.

Justin shook his head. Meg noticed he had refilled his glass. "I'm useless. I mean, here's the real story — the good guys and the bad guys facing off in the small town. And the whole thing is connected to what happened weeks ago. It'd be a good movie, in the right director's hands. But me? There's a hot story up the hill and I'm scared to go watch, even from a safe distance. I think I need to rethink some things."

"Well, right now you can keep me from falling apart. That's my unarmed husband up the hill, but I wouldn't even try to make him stay away."

"He's a better man than I am."

You've got that right, Justin, Meg said to herself.

27

The next surprise was the arrival of Lydia, who drove into the driveway and stopped abruptly. Meg had the door open before Lydia had climbed out of the car.

Lydia called out, "Did Art go up the hill?"

"He did. And so did Detective Marcus. And Seth. And Larry. What are you doing here?"

"Seth went?" Lydia asked, ignoring Meg's question.

"Yes. He said it was his house and he thought he should be there."

"But . . . guns!" Lydia said.

"I know. Did you hear any more shots?" When Lydia shook her head, Meg told her, "Maybe they ran out of ammunition. Maybe they were taking potshots at squirrels. Or maybe everybody's dead and there's nothing to worry about." Her sarcasm seemed to be escalating.

"Please, no! I refuse to consider that. But

we're worrying anyway, right?" Lydia responded.

"Of course. Christopher wasn't around?"

"No, or he'd have been up there alongside them. We don't spend *all* our time together."

"Seems like more and more. Which I think is great. You want a drink? We're working our way through a bottle of Scotch. Marcus included."

"Maybe one. A small one." By now they were in the kitchen, and Lydia spied Justin at the dining room table. "What's he doing here?"

"Justin? You know him?"

"I've seen him going into Seth's house a few times. Who is he?"

"A journalist, or so he thinks. He worked with Jenn in Boston. Or he works at the paper in Boston where Jenn used to work, which is not exactly the same thing. He knew her, and he was kind of following her hoping to get a piece of her big story."

"Yet here he sits, while the story takes place up the hill," Lydia said. "Maybe he should reconsider his career choice."

"That's what I told him." Meg handed Lydia a glass half filled with Scotch.

"Oh, my. I'll have to ask someone to drive me home if I finish this."

"We've got spare beds, if it comes to that."

Lydia took a healthy swallow of her drink. "I bet the drug police in Northampton are not going to be happy campers, if Detective Marcus and Art have taken the lead here. Unless they insist on prettying up the whole story to make their unit look good."

"I hope it's too late to try that. I'm pretty sure Marcus is fed up with their attitude. And Art has a legitimate reason to investigate suspicious gunshots in his own town."

Lydia took another cautious sip of her drink before asking, "Meg, do you have any reason to think that whatever was going on in that house was the main center of the local drug trade? Or was it just the tip of the iceberg?"

"Lydia, I don't know. I never knew what was going on up there. I guess I'm going to have to see things differently from now on. That or never leave the orchard." *And maybe wear a bulletproof vest in case of stray bullets?*

"I hope we can shut down this drug problem quickly," Lydia said. "Granford may be small and dull, but there are good people here. I don't think they deliberately turned a blind eye to what was happening — it's only that they didn't recognize it. However this all turns out, I think we've lost a bit of our innocence."

"I know. Maybe I should just introduce you to Justin and let him salvage a bit of his ego by interviewing you. Maybe he can get a human interest story out of it — you know, 'I Lived Next Door to a Drug Den.' Preferably after someone else breaks the story. He doesn't deserve it."

"It'll work as a distraction, while we wait."

"Follow me, then." She led Lydia into the dining room. "Justin, this is Seth's mother, Lydia. She lives in the house just down the road from Seth's house. She's the person who noticed the increase in traffic along that road."

Justin stood up politely. "It's nice to meet you, Mrs. Chapin. There seem to be a lot of Chapins in this neighborhood."

"Call me Lydia. Yes, there were Chapins here before there was a town, since the later eighteenth century. Are you interested in local history?"

The conversation that followed had an unreal quality. Meg's attention was divided between Justin and Lydia's superficial exchange of Granford facts and straining to hear any noise from up the hill — gunshots, sirens, bombs, or anything else. She was worried, despite the presence of two trained and armed law enforcement officials in the mix. But Seth? He was emotionally involved in stopping whatever was going on up there. It was his property, plus he was protecting his mother and his wife — her. Meg wondered which order she would like to see him put those in. If Jenn's body had been found on the other side of town, would he have cared as much? The councilman/friend-of-Art part of him would have been concerned, but she could have sat with him in front of the fire in their safe, comfortable home and commented on how sad and distressing it was. When it was a comfortable distance away.

"Was that a siren?" Meg asked, after what seemed like an hour of waiting but which was likely much less than that.

"I don't know," Lydia said.

Meg swallowed her next thought, so as not to alarm Lydia: if the guys had managed to settle things themselves, would they have needed backup sweeping in with sirens blaring? Or maybe it was the drug unit, miffed at being shut out, and trying to make the bust more dramatic than it actually was. Meg had to admit she simply didn't know much about police procedure, apart from the strictly local aspects like dog licenses and littering. Maybe Art and Marcus had conspired to arrest all of the occupants of the place — and any unlucky visitors they might have had — and needed to take them to Northampton to interview them. Or maybe it was an ambulance siren, because those earlier shots might have connected with someone. How long did it take an ambulance to arrive from the nearest hospital? Meg didn't know. She'd rather not know.

Maybe she should start dinner, since racing up the hill to satisfy her own curiosity was definitely not a good idea. She went hunting for a recipe that didn't require any thinking or attention and could serve a lot of people. Stew. Some kind of stew. Again. What did she have to work with? A foil-wrapped lump of mystery meat in the freezer. A half-full bag of potatoes, only slightly sprouted. Carrots. Herbs? And if it came up short, she could make dumplings. It was a plan of sorts, and would keep her busy. "I'm going to start dinner," she announced.

"Need some help?" Lydia volunteered. Maybe she'd had enough of trying to maintain a conversation with Justin, who seemed to be wallowing in self-recrimination — or frustration at having blown his big chance. Meg did not foresee a glorious career in journalism for the man.

"You up for peeling stuff?" Meg asked.

"Fine. Anything to keep busy." Lydia found an apron hanging on one of the kitchen doors and set to work on the potatoes with a peeler.

Justin did not volunteer to help — he was in a funk.

Meg lost track of time, but the stew was assembled and cooking in a slow oven when Meg finally heard voices. She glanced at Lydia. "They sound pleased with themselves." *As in, nobody is hurt or dead,* Meg added silently to herself.

"They do. I'll let them in."

Max, who had been dozing on the kitchen floor, beat her to the door, barking. He seemed excited too. Then Lydia pulled the kitchen door open and the kitchen was suddenly filled with large men with booming voices. They shucked off their winter coats and then they were smaller but no less loud — and apparently very pleased with themselves, as Meg had guessed.

Seth gave his mother a quick hug, then crossed the room to Meg, standing by the stove, and gave her a longer, bigger, better hug.

"Everything all right?" she asked. "We heard shots."

"Nobody got hurt," Seth told her. "We arrested the three guys at the house, all of them. The gunshots you heard were fired after someone tried to rip off the dealer — that'd be Ed. A buyer, or a competitor, grabbed a wad of cash and made a break for it. Ed blew out one of his tires as he peeled out of the driveway and he hit a tree, but he wasn't going very fast, so he wasn't really hurt. If you heard the ambulance, that was more a precaution, in case he was worse off than he looked. Are you okay?"

Meg nodded, waiting for the lump in her throat to clear. "I started cooking. Dinner will be ready sometime." In a lower voice she asked, "Why is Marcus still here? Didn't he want to go back to Northampton with his prisoners to bask in glory and thumb his nose at his narcotics colleagues?"

"Yes, and he will, but there's one piece of unfinished business. Is Justin still here?"

"Yes, in the front room. I think he's sulking, and he's been drinking pretty steadily. Why?"

"He's about to get a surprise." Seth turned to Marcus. "He's here. You ready?"

"Definitely," Marcus replied. He turned and strode into the front parlor, where Justin was sprawled in a shabby armchair. "Justin Campbell," Marcus began, "I'm arresting you on suspicion of acting as accessory before the fact in inciting the death of

Jenn Chambers."

It took Justin a moment before he could focus his eyes. "What? What'd I do?"

"We have arrested the other occupants of the house up the hill, and one of them gave you up."

Justin made an effort to stand, but it took a couple of tries. "I didn't do anything to Jenn. I barely even saw her here in Granford."

"That may be, but you told Ed Lopes that she was planning a story about the drug trade."

"Why would I do that?"

"Mr. Lopes didn't go into details, but I'm figuring it was because you wanted the story for yourself. You were pretending to be a buyer, but you told him you recognized her from a photo in the paper. With Jenn dead, you could write the article and lead with her heroic efforts and then go on with the story she would have written — only your name would be at the top, right? And the narcotics unit would go along with it, because no doubt you could portray them as heroes."

"And you're going to believe a lowlife like Ed Lopes instead of me? I wasn't even there!"

"He checked out your story and found

the picture. We have reason to believe that you met the dealers before Jenn introduced herself into their midst. And you came back once she had wormed her way in to tell them that she was about to blow up their whole business."

"Why would they believe me?" Justin protested.

"Maybe they didn't at first, but based on your comments they found out you were right. And then they gave some thought to what to do with her, and she ended up dead. So you, Justin Campbell, were indirectly responsible for getting her killed. That makes you an accomplice to murder. Jenn was careful, and the others might never have known who she really was without your tip."

"But . . . but . . ." Justin seemed to be at a loss for words. He really thought he'd gotten away with it? Meg wondered. Selfish, stupid young jerk. Thank goodness Marcus had nabbed him.

Marcus was still talking. "It may take a while to sort this mess out, but your pal Ed was pretty clear about how it happened. By the way, he says you still owe him money for your last buy."

"Do you know who my father is?" Justin demanded.

"No, and I don't really care, but I'm sure

you'll tell me. In any case, we took the time to alert our scruffy local press, and they've taken lots of pictures. They might even share the story with the *Globe,* since there's the connection with Jenn."

"And I think I know the right person to write it," Meg added with satisfaction: Toby would appreciate the boost, if the editors allowed him to run with the story. She almost felt sorry for Justin, just a bit. He thought he'd had things all worked out, and he'd been undercut by a couple of country cops and some amateurs. That must hurt. She had no idea who his father might be, but Daddy wasn't going to be very happy with his baby boy tonight.

"Anybody who wants to stay to dinner is welcome," Meg announced.

Marcus replied first, surprisingly warmly. "Thanks for the invitation, but I've got to get back to Northampton and start the paperwork. Rain check?"

"I'd like that, Detective. Just let me know when."

After he had gone, only the four of them were left, and Lydia and Larry had remained silent for most of the big reveal.

"Well," Lydia said, and stopped.

"My sentiments exactly," Meg replied. "Are you staying?"

"Why not? Christopher has a meeting this evening, although he'll want the full details later."

"Larry, what about you?"

"Okay. If you want me here."

"Of course we do. It probably hasn't sunk in yet, but you played a big part in sorting this out. You kept your promise to Jenn, but you trusted us to do the right thing with the information. I hope Marcus is impressed — if he isn't, I'll beat some sense into him."

Larry finally smiled. "Don't get yourself in trouble with him, Meg. Quit while you're ahead."

28

Once Meg had dished up the stew, every-one sat and started talking all at once. "So, Marcus arrested the right people," Seth began. "And I'm pretty sure he'll get a chunk of the credit for it, not just the narcotics people."

"I hate to say it, because it sounds kind of petty, but I'm really glad he arrested Justin. Justin didn't seem to realize he was playing with other people's lives, even after Jenn died. Completely self-centered. I hope he does some jail time."

"No, you're not vindictive, not at all," Seth remarked.

"Hey, I saw through him before you did," Meg shot back. "You know, we kind of skipped over some of the details, in the excitement of the arrest. What was the story with the original shooting?"

"As I understand it, it was kind of stupid, or the guys were getting a lot sloppier. They didn't think they had anything to worry about from the neighbors — that would be us — and they really believed they'd gotten away with murder," Seth said.

"So they shot Jenn and planted her where she would probably be found, as a warning to the competition?"

"Something like that."

"They weren't very smart. Whose gun was it?"

"Ed's. Unregistered, of course," Seth said.

"Did we get any parts of the story right?"

"We did. At least the basic outlines. There'll be more to come when Marcus and the narcotics guys track down some of the license plates, which should give some hint of where the drugs are coming from and who's buying them."

"So everything — everyone — really is all right?"

"Yes, it is."

"Try not to do that again, okay, Seth? I know why you wanted to be part of the confrontation, but maybe we could find a way to live a slightly more peaceful life?"

He smiled. "I would like that. But remember: this kind of trouble seems to keep finding us. It's not like we go looking for it. And if this mess has been of any use at all, it's proved that we can't simply ignore trouble because we don't want to see it or do anything about it."

"I do realize that. Why do you think we have a pair of goats? I didn't want them to be turned into somebody's dinner just because they were inconvenient."

"Exactly."

Larry seemed to have retreated into himself again, so Meg asked, "Larry, are you okay?"

"I think I will be. I'm not good at this kind of thing, but I want to say something. First, thank you for believing in me. I wasn't sure the police would, but you made a difference. Second, it really mattered to me that Jenn trusted me too. I know it might look like I was the only person she thought she could count on up at the house, which wasn't exactly a compliment, but she believed I'd do the right thing."

"Good." Meg felt a tangled knot deep inside her unravel. It really was over? Maybe Granford would never look quite the same in her eyes, but the good guys had won, and life would go on. And people might just pay a little more attention to what was going on in their peaceful town.

"It really looks great," Meg said to Larry as she admired the tiny house, now close to finished. "And it came together so quickly! Are you happy with the results?"

"Yeah, pretty much," Larry said, more or less smiling. "I know I could stay on at Seth's house, but after what happened, I'm just not comfortable there, and I don't want to keep hiding out in my room or looking over my shoulder all the time."

"I understand. You're a private person, and there's nothing wrong with that. This is yours, for as long as you want it, and if Seth wants to show it off to potential clients, he'll have to get your permission first."

"Good to know. But . . . after what happened with Jenn, I found out that I need some space for other things. We weren't exactly, well, physical, but I wouldn't have felt right with all those other people coming and going all the time, even if it had happened."

"I understand, Larry. I'm glad you and Jenn hit it off, and that she felt she could trust you."

"Yeah, that mattered. I know it wouldn't have lasted, because she had a job in Boston, but I'm glad I met her. What's happening with her article?"

"You mean, now that Justin's lost his job and is waiting for his trial? I'm hoping Toby will have a chance to step up and take over.

He knew Jenn, and he's been at the paper for a while. I think he could do a good job. It should happen soon, anyway, and I'm pretty sure his name will be somewhere on it."

"Good to know. You ready to get back to the orchard?"

"I thought you'd never ask. Here's hoping we have a good year!"

ABOUT THE AUTHOR

After collecting too many degrees and exploring careers ranging from art historian to investment banker to professional genealogist, **Sheila Connolly** began writing mysteries in 2001 and is now a full-time writer.

She wrote her first mystery series for Berkley Prime Crime under the name Sarah Atwell, and the first book, *Through a Glass, Deadly,* was nominated for an Agatha Award for Best First Novel.

Under her own name, her Orchard Mystery Series debuted with *One Bad Apple* and has been followed by twelve more books in the series.

Her Museum Mysteries, set in the Philadelphia museum community, opened with *Fundraising the Dead* and continued with seven more books.

Her County Cork Mysteries debuted with

Buried in a Bog, followed by five more novels.

She has also published numerous original ebooks with Beyond the Page: *Sour Apples, Once She Knew, The Rising of the Moon, Reunion with Death, Under the Hill, Relatively Dead, Seeing the Dead, Defending the Dead, Watch for the Dead, Search for the Dead,* and *Revealing the Dead.*

Sheila is a member of Sisters in Crime, Mystery Writers of America, and Romance Writers of America. She is a former President of Sisters in Crime New England, and was cochair for the 2011 New England Crime Bake conference.